We ran through the snow at the side of the road until we were out of breath; I was sure the shots would bring a Russian patrol. We'd leave tracks in the snow but we'd have made more noise in the hard-packed center of the road. The end of the snowstorm had brought that still, bitter cold when a running step echoes like hammer on anvil.

We heard the guard's carbine blast the padlock off the gate. We started to run again, and the siren went off; there must have been a switch in the sentry box. We heard the sound of a car coming toward us and saw the long beams of the headlights slashing into the shadows of the trees at the bend in the road ahead. The rising scream of the siren and the moving light and the throb of the car's engine seemed to freeze us where we stood...

PASSPORT *to* PERIL

by **Robert B. Parker**

A HARD CASE **HARD CASE CRIME** CRIME NOVEL

A HARD CASE CRIME BOOK
(HCC-057)
July 2009

Published by

Dorchester Publishing Co., Inc.
200 Madison Avenue
New York, NY 10016

in collaboration with Winterfall LLC

ISBN 0-8439-6119-8
ISBN-13 978-0-8439-6119-5

Cover design by Cooley Design Lab

Typeset by Swordsmith Productions

The name "Hard Case Crime" and the Hard Case Crime logo
are trademarks of Winterfall LLC. Hard Case Crime books are
selected and edited by Charles Ardai.

Printed in the United States of America

Visit us on the web at www.HardCaseCrime.com

For my children

PASSPORT TO PERIL

Chapter One
FRIGHTENED GIRL

It wasn't until the Orient Express was nearing the Hungarian frontier, about two hours out of Vienna, that I found I was traveling on the passport of a murdered man.

I'd been alone in my compartment for most of the time, reading the Budapest papers and planning my mission to Hungary, my first visit since the end of the war. It was good to be in the luxurious international train. Snow had fallen heavily since we'd pulled out of the Westbahnhof in Vienna, and there was a biting north wind.

The girl entered the compartment just after the Orient had flashed through the bombed-out ruins of Bruck-an-der-Leithe. I had wiped the mist off the window and was watching the station lights flicker through the falling snow. At first I thought the door had been opened by the Wagons-Lits porter or the dining-car steward to tell me dinner was ready. Then I heard a woman's voice say in French, "Thank god you're here. I thought you'd been—"

I'll always remember that warm, low voice. It

stopped abruptly when I turned to show my face. The girl was tall and slender, somewhere in her middle twenties.

"I'm terribly sorry. I've made a mistake." She turned her head to check the number on the compartment door. "No, this *is* number seven, isn't it?" She glanced at the baggage rack above my head. When she looked at me there was complete disbelief in the dark face. "I thought you were someone else." She paused. "You even look a great deal like him."

"Perhaps you're in the wrong car," I said. "Are you sure you want car twenty-two?"

"Yes, car twenty-two." She pointed to the rack. "That's my baggage. I put it there before we left the station." She took her ticket from her pocket and studied it. "Compartment seven, car twenty-two. There's no mistake."

I checked my ticket again, and it was correct. There are two seats in a second-class compartment when the sleeping-car is used for daytime travel.

There was bewilderment in the girl's wide-set black eyes. I found her extremely attractive. Her raven-black hair was parted and drawn behind her ears, and her cheeks were a little hollowed so that her cheekbones and the firm line of her jaw showed clearly. She was wearing a gray tweed suit with a frilly blouse and she carried a blue velvet beret in her hand.

She hesitated, and for a moment I thought she would leave the compartment, but she finally sat beside me, and I offered her the Hungarian newspapers. "No, thank you. I'm afraid I don't read Hungarian." The puzzled light was still in her eyes. She turned to me. "Would you mind telling me how you got this seat?"

"Not at all. It's very simple. The Wagons-Lits office in Vienna swore the Orient was sold out. But I've usually found that at least one person fails to show up at the station. I took a chance and got aboard. This was the only vacant seat, and I bought it from the porter after the train started."

The girl was quiet a moment, as if she were trying to imagine what had caused the other man to miss the train, the man whose seat I'd taken. "Is there another train tonight from Vienna to Budapest?"

"I don't think so," I said. "There's a local tomorrow morning. But there's the Russian plane tonight. It gets to Budapest before we do." I didn't want to frighten her but I couldn't help adding, "It isn't very safe. I wouldn't want to take it in this weather. The pilot hedgehops all the way to follow the tracks." I was about to tell her of the trip I'd made in a Russian plane from Budapest to Bucharest with the pilot using an oil company's road map to guide him, but something in her expression told me she wasn't in the mood for levity.

The girl said, "Have you ever been to Budapest?" even though she'd seen me reading the Hungarian newspapers. Maybe she thought I'd picked up the language at Berlitz.

"Yes," I said, "I was living in Budapest when the war started. I know it very well. It's the most beautiful city in the world—or it was before the Germans and the Russians blew it apart."

She accepted a cigarette from my case, and I lit it. I asked her if she knew Budapest. She shook her head, and I noticed the blue highlights in the midnight-black of her hair. "Not at all," she said. "I've never been in this part of Europe before." I wondered about her nationality. Her French was grammatically perfect, but the accent was off somewhere.

"Could I get back to Vienna tonight? Could I get a train from the border?"

Maybe she was on her honeymoon. That would account for her distress. But there weren't any rings on her long, slender fingers.

I knew there weren't any trains from the frontier that night—I'd learned the timetable by heart—but I felt sorry for her. I said, "Let's look it up. There must be a railway guide in the porter's compartment. I'll get it."

I opened the door and bumped into a man in the corridor. I excused myself and he grunted, but he didn't move and I had to wedge past him. He was leaning on the rail, apparently engrossed in watching the melting snowflakes slide down the heated glass. I didn't pay much attention to him except to notice he was short and squat, with a bullet head that could have made him almost any nationality in Central Europe.

The railway guide, which I took back to the compartment, showed the westbound Orient had already passed us on its run to the English Channel. The only train back to Vienna would leave Budapest at six the following morning and the frontier station shortly after ten.

The girl bit her lip. "Is there a place where I could spend the night at the border?" Her long fingers were twisting and untwisting a lace handkerchief in her lap.

"I'm afraid there isn't," I said. "Hegyshalom, the border town, is a pretty primitive place." I added, "But they wouldn't let you off the train, anyway. The whole area is a Russian military zone."

I thought I saw something close to despair in her black eyes. It made me say, "I don't think you ought to worry. I'll be glad to escort you to your hotel. You can send a telegram to Vienna. You can telephone, I think, if it's important enough."

She stood up and went over to the window and looked out for a minute or two without speaking. Then she turned and left the compartment.

I figured I had troubles enough of my own without looking for more. I picked up one of the Budapest papers which carried a piece I wanted to read again on the Hungarian steel industry but I'd scarcely scanned the first paragraph when the girl came back. She slammed the door and drew the bolt, and when she sat beside me I saw that her face was white and drawn. She ran a distracted hand through her hair. She wiped the palms of her hands with her handkerchief. It was a little while before her breathing became normal. I pretended to be reading but I watched her out of the corner of my eye.

In a minute or two, she turned to me and said in a

thin voice, "I don't know what you must think. I guess you must think—"

There was a knock on the door, sharp and insistently repeated. I put down my paper and started to get up, but the girl grabbed my sleeve. There was terror in her big black eyes.

"Please," she said, "please don't open it. Please, you mustn't. You'll help me, won't you? Tell me you'll help me."

"Of course I'll help you," I said. "But we can't stay in here with the door bolted."

"Something terrible will happen if you open that door. You mustn't."

I started getting fed up at that point. I could understand a girl being upset and overwrought because her husband or her lover had missed a train. But I couldn't see why that was any reason to ignore knocking at the door.

"Nonsense," I said. I got up and slid back the bolt. I saw the girl had moved out of her seat and was standing behind me. I opened the door.

"Beg pardon, sir. Will you have first or second sitting at dinner, sir? First sitting when the train clears the Hungarian frontier, second sitting an hour later, sir."

When I had closed the door, I saw that the girl had buried her face in her hands. I sat beside her and said as evenly as I could, "What's this all about? There's no reason to be afraid of the dining-car steward. What were you saying when he knocked?"

She didn't look up but she said, "I was saying I can't imagine what you must think of me."

I had begun to suspect she was a girl with too much imagination and too little control of herself but I didn't say so. I said, "I think you're letting yourself get hysterical over nothing. Lots of people travel alone. You're perfectly safe in this train. You've got to take hold of yourself."

The girl said, "It isn't traveling alone. I'm not worried about that. I've traveled lots of times alone."

I offered her a cigarette, but she shook her head. I said, "Then what is there to worry about? Come on, forget it. I've got tickets for the first sitting. I think I can talk the porter into getting us a cocktail if you'd like."

She dabbed at her eyes with the handkerchief. She said, "I'm sorry. I don't see why I should expect you to understand." She put her hand on my arm. "You see it's just that I'm terribly afraid."

I don't imagine I sounded very sympathetic. "I can see that," I said. "But you haven't anything to be afraid of. Nobody will hurt you in Budapest. You must have been reading a lot of wild stories. I told you I'll be glad to take you to your hotel. I'll be glad to look after you until your friend arrives. If he doesn't take the plane, he'll certainly come on the morning train. I'm sure you'll find a message from him when you get to the hotel in Budapest."

"That's very kind of you," the girl said. "But it isn't a friend who's missing. It's my employer. I'm his secretary."

"Okay," I said. "Then it's your employer. I'll be glad to look after you until your employer arrives."

She shook her head. "He isn't going to arrive in Budapest at all."

"Why not? Is he afraid to travel alone, too?"

The girl raised her head and looked me straight in the eye.

"He isn't coming to Budapest," she said evenly. "He isn't coming because he's been murdered in Vienna."

If she wasn't a lunatic, she was dangerously close to it. I decided to leave her and go into the dining car for a drink.

"Oh, you can think I'm crazy but I know what I'm talking about. My employer was murdered all right. The man who killed him is right outside this door. He was in the corridor when I went out. I know he killed my employer. Now he's following me."

I opened the door. The corridor was empty.

I decided to give one last try. "You mustn't get hysterical. You're letting your imagination run away with you. Lots of people miss trains every day. That doesn't mean they've been murdered."

It was so much wasted breath.

"Oh, I do know what I'm saying," the girl went on. There was a wild light in her deep, black eyes. "You think I'm crazy, don't you? You think I'm good for the madhouse, don't you? I don't blame you. But my employer told me he'd be killed in Vienna. He told me that man outside would kill him."

"But there's no one outside," I insisted.

The girl shook her head. "My employer told me that on the train. I saw that man following us. My employer pointed him out to me on the train from Geneva."

I must have shown surprise at the word Geneva because Geneva was now supposed to be my home town. At least, that's what it said in the passport I was carrying in my pocket. I must have shown surprise in my face, because the girl quickly picked it up.

"You aren't from Geneva, are you?" She said it eagerly, as if in her highly excited state she wanted to find some link with the familiar.

I decided I might just as well start playing my role, the part I'd planned for my visit to Hungary. I was about to leave her to go into the dining car anyway.

I said yes I came from Geneva.

"Then maybe you knew my employer?" The deliberate use of the past tense sent the chills up and down my spine.

"Perhaps I did," I said. If it would help to calm her there was no harm in pretending I'd heard of the man in a business way. I might even convince her I'd seen him alive in Vienna if that would quiet her nerves for the rest of the trip. I couldn't expect to stay in the dining car the whole way to Budapest. I'd have to return to the compartment and to her at some point.

I added casually, "What was his name?" I had stood up, and my hand was on the door handle when she answered.

"Marcel Blaye," she said. "B-L-A-Y-E. Oh, then you did know him?"

If you've ever experienced the sickening sensation of a sudden, unending drop in an abandoned elevator you'll know how I felt. I'm sure my eyes started from my head. I felt drops of perspiration stand out on my forehead. I choked on my cigarette but I managed to stammer, "I've heard of Monsieur Blaye." It seemed a long time before I recovered myself enough to sit down and turn my face to the window.

You see, Marcel Blaye was the name on the Swiss passport which I had bought for $500 that morning in Vienna. I had thought I was getting a clever forgery, even to the Hungarian visa which the Russians had consistently refused me as John Stodder, American. I had taken for granted that Marcel Blaye of Geneva was a figment of the forger's imagination. I had complimented Herr Figl on the quick job he'd done, even to the ugly red stain on the cover which made the passport look used.

The girl had said, "You even look a great deal like him," when she'd first entered the compartment. That explained the similarity in statistics—the same height, six feet, the same weight, 178 pounds, the same black hair and brown eyes, even a similar scar on the upper right cheek. The age on the passport was thirty-five, two years older than I. Figl had said it was a meaningless error in transcribing from the notes I'd given him the night before. In reality, all the filthy Austrian had done was to change the photograph. He'd stolen the passport from Marcel Blaye's corpse.

I don't know how long we sat in silence before I glanced at my watch. Fifteen—no, fourteen minutes to Hegyshalom, the Hungarian border station. There would be a general alarm at all frontiers for the murderer of Marcel Blaye, for the man who had killed him in Vienna and robbed him of his passport.

I stood up and faced the girl. "Listen," I said. "I believe you. Don't ask me why but I know you're telling the truth. I'm going to help you. You've got to trust me. We've got to leave this train."

There wasn't any time to tell her my story. She wouldn't have believed it anyway. She'd have thought I was in league with the man in the corridor. How else could I have received Marcel Blaye's passport—and his seat on the Orient Express?

I opened the door an inch, ready to slam and bolt it again, but the corridor was deserted. I turned to tell the girl to follow me and saw her standing on the seat, reaching into the baggage rack. I started to say we couldn't take any baggage until I saw she had fished a fat Manila envelope from a suitcase. She could stick that in her pocket; we'd have to abandon everything else.

She followed me through the darkened corridors. When we neared the end of the last car, I whispered to her to wait until I called.

I walked to the end of the corridor. There was a Russian guard on the back platform, a carbine slung over his shoulder, his face nearly hidden by the collar of his greatcoat.

I went into the toilet, locked the door, and took the roll of paper from the hook. I unrolled the paper until it made a heap in the corner. Then I touched my lighter to the pile. I unlocked the door and went to the platform.

"Fire," I said to the guard in Russian. "There's fire in the toilet. The train is on fire."

He slowly took the carbine from his shoulder, leaned

it against the vestibule wall and then walked deliberately past me into the corridor, without a word. I watched him go into the toilet. When he'd shut the door, I waved to the girl to come to the platform. We could hear him splashing water from the basin onto the blazing paper.

The train was moving slowly, climbing steadily. The smoke from the laboring engine swirled onto the platform.

"Jump," I told the girl. She landed in the drifted snow piled high alongside the track.

I tossed the guard's carbine. Then I jumped.

For a moment after I landed in the snow I thought I might have set too big a blaze. Suppose the whole wooden coach caught fire? The guard was patently stupid but not too stupid to pull the alarm signal. The Orient would grind to a stop. It wouldn't take long to start a dozen armed guards looking for us.

I called to the girl who was twenty feet or so away from me. I told her to lie quiet. In a minute, I lifted myself to one knee. The train was no longer in sight. When I heard the faint, faraway moan of the locomotive, I got to my feet and went to help the girl. I found the carbine and brushed off the wet snow.

The tracks were hedged in on both sides by towering pines. The storm had lifted, and far up the tracks we could see the first stars.

I made sure the carbine was loaded and the trigger set. I told the girl to follow and started up the tracks in the direction the train had gone.

I didn't have the slightest idea what to do next. I was only glad that I wasn't going to be on the Orient when the Hungarian police came aboard and that neither the girl nor I would have to face the squat little murderer with the bullet head.

Chapter Two
DESPERATE FLIGHT

We walked the ties for more than a mile before we came to a break in the pines—and then we found ourselves on a Russian military road. It didn't take long for us to wish we'd taken our chances on the train.

We had spoken only once during the uphill walk, when the girl caught her breath long enough to ask me if Vienna wasn't in the other direction. I said we were following the train only because the sky was clearer in that direction. "We aren't walking to Vienna." I put out my hand. "I think it's high time we were introduced. My name is John Stodder."

"And mine is Maria Torres," the girl said. There was enough light from the stars for me to see she was smiling. There was no sign of the panic she'd shown on the train. It was hard going for her along the ties; she was wearing high heels and she'd tripped once but she didn't complain.

We turned into the plowed side road but we hadn't gone far when I heard a car approaching from the direction of the railroad. I pulled Maria off the road into the shadow of the pines. We watched a big Russian military car lumber through the deep ruts, heard it skid to a stop a few hundred feet beyond us, then grind off again in low gear a minute later.

When we could no longer hear the car's engine, we walked slowly alone the side of the road until we came in sight of a gate in a high wire fence which crossed the road. I whispered to Maria to wait while I moved up to the fence. The gate was chained and locked. There was no way to scale the fence, which was topped with barbed wire. There was a sentry box on the other side, off the road, but it was empty, and there were tracks in the snow where the sentry had gone into the woods. Apparently he had just started his tour, after opening and closing the gate for the car.

I was sure he'd be gone ten or fifteen minutes and there was nothing to do until he returned. Perhaps I could think of a way to trick him into unlocking the gate. I took Maria's arm, and we moved back to a rock in the shadow of the trees, just short of the fence. Maria sat beside me. She was shivering with cold, and I made her take my overcoat. I cupped a match in my hands to light cigarettes.

Maria said, "How long before they start looking for us?"

I couldn't see her face, but her voice was steady.

"Daylight," I said. I tried to sound offhand. "There isn't much they can do tonight." I was sure the military car had been searching for us but I didn't want to alarm her. The car could have been alerted by shortwave radio from the train.

"You're sure they'll look for us?"

"Yes," I said. I couldn't fool her to that extent. "In

the morning. By that time we'll be back in Vienna. It can't be more than seventy kilometers."

"What are we going to do now?"

"First we're going to get through this gate. Then we're going to find a farmer with a car or a truck to take us to Vienna. I've plenty of dollars. There's always someone in these countries who'll do anything for dollars." I wished I had been as confident as I hoped I sounded. I thought of my green American passport, locked in the safe at the Hotel Bristol in Vienna.

Maria's low voice cut into my thoughts. "They'll know who we are from our baggage, won't they?" That was just the trouble. I'd very carefully changed the labels on my bags and in my clothing that morning in Vienna. I'd marked everything with the name Marcel Blaye and the address Geneva. Proof to any policeman that I'd robbed Blaye after killing him.

The girl's cigarette glowed in the dark. She said, "I've led you into a lot of trouble. I don't know why I let you do this for me."

I couldn't tell her the whole truth, not before we were safely back in Vienna. So I told her half the truth. "I happen to like you. And I've been in trouble myself." Then I said, "Who was Marcel Blaye?" The past tense no longer seemed out of place.

Maria said, "I'm not very sure that I know." She paused, and I waited for her to go on. Somewhere in the distance an owl hooted, and from time to time the limb of a tree would crack like a rifle bullet under the weight of the newly fallen snow.

"Monsieur Blaye described himself as an exporter

of watches and clocks. He had an office in Geneva, off the Rue du Mont Blanc near the post office. He came to Geneva just before the end of the war—early in 1945, I think. You see, I don't know very much about him because I only worked for him six weeks."

"You mean you didn't know very much about him, yet you were willing to travel with him to Budapest?"

Maria was silent for a moment. "I don't think you can understand unless I explain the background. It's just that I have three younger sisters to support." She stubbed her cigarette in the snow and pulled my coat closer about her shoulders. "When we were children, we lived in Madrid, where we were born. My father was a lawyer but he was also a republican and when the monarchy was overthrown, he became Spanish consul to Geneva. When Franco made his revolt, my father insisted on returning to Spain to fight. He was killed at Guadalajara."

I listened, but there was no sound of the sentry returning.

"The Republic took care of Mother and us until it ceased to exist. Mother worked at the League of Nations for a while but she died of pneumonia when I was seventeen. I've been working ever since. I went to work for Monsieur Blaye just because he offered a lot more money than I was making at the time."

I found myself wondering what interest Blaye had taken in Maria Torres.

"He wasn't interested in me, if that's what you're thinking," she said. "I never knew him before I answered his ad in the *Journal de Geneve*. He seemed to be very much in love with a Polish girl, a Countess Orlovska, who used to come to the office."

"Why were you going to Budapest?"

"Monsieur Blaye said he'd arranged a big deal with the Hungarian government. He said it was so important and so secret that I mustn't say a word to anyone. He even made me tell my sisters that we were only going to Zurich."

"What about the man on the train? Who is he?"

"He told me his name was Doctor Schmidt," Maria said, "but I don't know much about him. I saw him for the first time a week ago when he came to the Geneva office. He and Monsieur Blaye had a terrible row in Monsieur's private room. The next time I saw him was on the train from Geneva."

"What did Blaye tell you about him?"

"Monsieur Blaye caught sight of Doctor Schmidt in the dining car. I thought Monsieur would die of fright. He left his dinner half eaten and insisted on locking himself in his compartment. That's when he told me Schmidt was planning to kill him."

I lit cigarettes for both of us and passed one to Maria.

"Monsieur Blaye insisted on leaving the train at Zurich and taking the next one. But it didn't do any good because Doctor Schmidt did the same thing. When we arrived in Vienna, Monsieur took me to the Metropole in a taxi. He gave me an envelope to carry and told me he'd meet me on the Orient this afternoon. That was the last I saw of him."

I figured Blaye must have been murdered shortly after leaving Maria. Herr Figl would have needed at

least twelve hours to substitute my photograph for
Blaye's and to forge a new Swiss foreign-office seal
for the picture, apparently the only change he had
needed to make.

"You aren't Swiss, are you?" Maria said.

Something told me to be cautious. "Why do you say
that?"

"Because," Maria said, "when you mentioned the
distance to Vienna, you said 'soixante-dix' the way a
Frenchman does. If you were Swiss you would have
said 'septente.' "

"As a matter of fact, I'm American," I said. The only
thing that mattered any longer was Blaye's passport.
There was no reason not to tell her the truth about
everything else.

"You speak French without an accent," the girl said.
"You must have lived in France."

"I was born in Paris," I told her. "My father was in
the American consular service for many years. We lived
all over the world. I never learned very much in school
but I did pick up languages."

"Are you a diplomat?"

I laughed. "No," I said, "I'm a newspaperman. After
college in America, I seemed to drift naturally into foreign correspondence, largely because of my languages
I guess."

"Then you're going to Budapest on assignment?"
Maria asked.

I hadn't talked to anybody about my reasons for
going to Budapest. My father and mother thought I
was still in Paris. The whole project was something I'd

kept locked inside me. It was a mission that had to be accomplished if I were to go on living with myself.

"I'm going to Hungary to look for a man," I said.

Maria was so close I could hear her breathing.

"It's a long story," I said, "and one I'm not very proud of. I don't think it would interest you." I found myself wanting desperately to tell her, this girl I'd known less than two hours and whom I'd probably never see again after we returned to Vienna. Because, as soon as I recovered my American passport, I'd have to find another way to enter Hungary.

I felt Maria's hand on my arm. "Please tell me," she said. "I want to hear it."

"I told you my father was in the consular service," I said. "There were five of us in the family—Father and Mother, of course, my sister Daphne, my brother Bob, and me. We were always very close as a family, perhaps because we shared the same experiences and because we lived so much in foreign surroundings.

"Bob and I were always together although he was"
—there was that damned past tense again—"although he was two years younger than I. When we were children Mother taught us together so that when we entered boarding-school in America we were in the same class. We went to college together and shared the same room for four years."

There was the sound of an airplane overhead, and we could see the running lights blinking against the stars. The Russian plane which wasn't carrying Marcel Blaye.

"After we graduated, I came to Europe for a news

agency, and Bob went on to law school. But I went home just before Pearl Harbor, and my brother and I enlisted in the Air Corps after America went into the war. We took our basic training together and went to Officer Candidate School. Then, because I had been a newspaperman, I was sent to Intelligence School while Bob became a navigator."

Now that the words were coming out, it was almost as if someone else were talking.

"Strangely enough, we wound up in the same heavy-bomber outfit. I say strange because the Air Corps usually went to lengths to separate brothers. Anyway, we went through the campaign in Italy and when that was cleaned up we were assigned to help the Russians. One of our first missions was to attack the Manfried Weiss steel works—they're on an island in the Danube at Budapest. They were producing for the Germans who had taken over Hungary."

I paused to relight my cigarette.

"Six planes went on the mission, and none of them came back. Oh, they accomplished their mission all right. They blasted hell out of the steel works, which stopped working for the Germans or anybody else. But the planes never got back to base. One crashed and the entire crew was killed. The other five either crash-landed or the crews bailed out. Most of them were captured and put in prison camps. A few escaped into Yugoslavia and joined the Partisans."

"What was wrong with the planes?" Maria asked.

"Nothing," I said, "except they ran out of gas. The operations office made a stupid, inexcusable miscalculation, and the airplanes arrived over the target more than an hour before daylight. The hour they had to circle above the clouds before attacking made the difference between having enough gas and what happened."

"What about your brother?" the girl said.

"He bailed out safely," I said. "The whole crew got out all right. They started walking to Yugoslavia and they made it—all except Bob. Somewhere along the line he disappeared. Neither the Air Corps nor the State Department has ever been able to find a trace of him. He just vanished into thin air."

Maria said, "I know how your family must feel. It must be terrible for all of you, the dreadful uncertainty, not knowing anything for sure. For a while we didn't know for sure about my father."

"Yes," I said, "and there's something even my family doesn't know. I was the officer who made the fatal mistake."

We heard the sentry returning through the woods, whistling. I told Maria to crouch behind the rock so that she wouldn't be seen from the road if the sentry should use a flashlight.

I ran down the road until I was out of sight of the gate. I raised the railway guard's carbine and squeezed three shots in quick succession. Then I ducked into the woods and doubled back to the fence as fast as I could move through the deep snow. I reached the fence in time to see the sentry open the padlock in the glare of his flashlight, slide through the gate, and run toward the spot from where I had fired. It didn't take me long to grab Maria's arm, hustle her through the gate, and snap the lock again.

We ran through the snow at the side of the road until we were out of breath; I was sure the shots would bring a Russian patrol. We'd leave tracks in the snow but we'd have made more noise in the hard-packed center of the road. The end of the snowstorm had brought that still, bitter cold when a running step echoes like hammer on anvil.

I suppose we'd put a hundred yards or so between us and the fence when we heard the guard's carbine blast the padlock off the gate. We started to run again, and the siren went off; there must have been a switch in the sentry box. We ran until Maria tripped, let go my hand, and fell heavily. I picked her up and we heard the sound of a car coming toward us and saw the long beams of the headlights slashing into the shadows of the trees at the bend in the road ahead. The rising scream of the siren and the moving light and the throb of the car's engine seemed to freeze us where we stood, locked in each other's arms.

Then I knew another sound. Somewhere close behind us there was a running brook. Our only chance to get a head start on the Russian patrol was to follow that brook into the woods. If we left the road through the snow they'd follow our tracks in a minute.

Luckily the icy water wasn't much above our ankles, and we were already numbed with the cold. We made good progress into the woods, following the center of the stream by the sound of the water alone. I looked back once, and the road was bright with the light of the oncoming car. The siren had died away. The roar of the car's engine and the rushing of the water beneath us were the only sounds.

When we were well into the woods, the going became harder without even the little light from the stars. I stumbled and fell half a dozen times before I sensed that Maria was no longer close behind me. I didn't dare call her. I turned back, putting my arms out straight in front of me the way a blind man does but I didn't find her. I tried using my lighter, but it was dripping wet.

I lost my head. I found myself trying to run through the stream, stumbling and crashing on my face when the stones on the bottom rolled under my feet, calling Maria's name at the top of my lungs.

Somehow I found her, down on her knees in the water. I picked her up in my arms and I knew she had fainted from exhaustion and the cold. I turned and went blindly forward again but slower so that I wouldn't fall with her.

I'll never know how far I walked before I knew there was a light ahead. My eyes must have seen it long before my brain accepted it.

Of course, when the Russians hadn't found us on the road, they'd doubled to the other side of the woods.

I put Maria down in the snow at the side of the brook, unslung the carbine from my shoulder, and started to knock off the safety. But I had no choice. I threw the gun upstream as far as my strength would let me. I picked up the girl again and started for the light. No matter what happened to me I had to get help for her.

When the light grew brighter and brighter, I tried to run through the snow. Then I heard a shout. I heard the crack of a rifle bullet. I felt my knees give way under me. And then nothing more.

Chapter Three
DOUBTFUL SAFETY

When I opened my eyes someone was bending over me. My first thought was to ask the Russians to take care of Maria, to tell them she was innocent and that I had forced her to leave the train with me.

I tried to lift myself on one elbow, fighting to clear my brain enough to recall the Russian words. But a hand pushed me back on the snow, and a voice said, "Warten Sie einen Augenblick, mein Herr—wait a minute."

For a moment I thought I must be delirious. I had expected to hear Russian. I wasn't prepared for German.

If these men proved to be Austrian police, we might have an easier time with them. There wasn't any love lost between the Austrians and the Red Army. Perhaps they weren't policemen at all. They might be farmers or hunters who could be persuaded to let us go in return for the dollars in my pocket.

The voice above me called out, "Er ist nicht verwundet," and another voice close by answered, "And neither is the girl. You're not the marksman you used to be, Otto."

"Hold your tongue," said Otto. "It's just as well I

didn't hit them. This man is carrying a Swiss passport.
And a wad of traveler's checks, too."

Why hadn't I destroyed Marcel Blaye's passport? I
could have thrown it away after leaving the train without exciting Maria's suspicion.

Otto raised his voice, apparently addressing a third
man who was some distance away. "Hermann, don't
stand there like a dunderhead with your mouth wide
open. Quick, go get help. Hurry."

I must have passed out again and for quite a time
because when I regained consciousness I was being
carried on a stretcher. I was wrapped in blankets, and
my wet clothes had been removed. I could raise my
head enough to see that Maria was on a stretcher ahead.

Then I heard Otto say, "Bring them in here. Quickly."
We were carried the length of a low wooden porch, then
lifted into a brightly lighted room. It was the main room
of a typical Central European hunting-lodge. A wood-
paneled room with a high peaked roof, huge stone fire-
places at both ends, heads of deer and bear and
mountain sheep on the walls, the rustic furniture. The
kind of room to which Austro-Hungarian aristocrats
repaired after the hunt, to wine and dine, gamble and
make love to the music of a gypsy band. Perhaps we
had been brought in by some rich man's gamekeepers,
if there were any rich men left other than commissars,
someone who might hate Communism enough to help
us get away. Otto and his helpers weren't in uniform.
They wore the short fur-lined jackets, the feathered
felt hats, and the high laced boots of the Austrian
countrymen.

They lifted me from the stretcher and carried me to a chair in the middle of the room. Otto stuck a glass of apricot brandy in my hand. Otto was a dark, mean-looking character, with a great black mustache and a patch over one eye.

"Where's the girl?" I said. "Is she all right? What have you done with her?"

"You speak German like a Berliner," Otto said. "The girl's all right. We put her to bed. You'll both be all right in the morning. It's lucky we found you. You might have spent the rest of your lives on crutches."

There were two doors at the far side of the room. I guessed they led to bedrooms, the kitchen, and the servants' quarters.

The room reminded me of a stage setting and it turned out to be just that. The cuckoo clock on the mantelpiece struck ten. Almost immediately, as if with the rising of a curtain, one of the doors on the far side opened, and a man entered. He was wearing a uniform, complete to gold epaulets and several rows of ribbons. It was a Russian uniform, and the wearer might have come off a Red Square parade. Otto and his helpers clicked their heels and snapped to attention. I should have remembered that the Red Army had recruited thousands of former Wehrmacht soldiers for guard duty in Central Europe. Germans like Otto knew no other trade. Just as their fathers had joined foreign armies after Imperial Germany's defeat in the First World War, so Otto and many like him were serving their Russian conquerors until they might again wear the uniform of a resurgent Reich.

The Russian made a stage bow in my direction as he closed the door, then in German banished Otto and the others from the room. He turned his back to the fireplace, locked his hands behind him, and bowed again. He was tall and thin, with graying hair and the bushiest pair of black eyebrows I'd ever seen.

"Good evening, Monsieur Blaye," he said in excellent French. "Please, you will permit me to introduce myself. I am Major Ivan Strakhov at your service, Monsieur."

Of course Otto had returned to the lodge with the passport before we'd arrived. Major Strakhov had addressed me as Monsieur Blaye for want of another name. He had no way of knowing I was John Stodder, American.

"I had expected the pleasure of welcoming you at the frontier, at Hegyshalom," he said with a broad smile. "I'm sorry you did not advise us you were planning to leave the Orient Express somewhat short of the station."

It was the major, then, in the military car which had passed us when we first turned off the railway tracks into the side road. The train guards had radioed to Hegyshalom as soon as we jumped.

"These German peasants aren't much good," he said, waving his hand in the direction in which Otto and his men had disappeared, "but it's lucky they found you. I'm afraid they were trying to jack deer with a lantern when you ran into them. They're just like children." It was the speech a German officer would have made about the Russians, a few years and one lost war earlier.

"I'm sorry to say, Monsieur Blaye, that your failure

to arrive at Hegyshalom proved a great disappointment to Countess Orlovska," the major continued. "She came with me from Budapest to meet you but she has returned to the capital in the Orient. She requested me to tell you that she looks forward eagerly to seeing you as soon as you arrive." He added in an offhand manner, "I must say I thought her somewhat upset when she heard you had brought your pretty secretary."

I was so tired and confused that I didn't catch on. I thought the major possessed an exceedingly macabre sense of humor. Maria had said that Blaye "seemed to be very much in love with a Polish girl, a Countess Orlovska, who used to come to the office." And what did Strakhov mean "as soon as you arrive"?

"Excuse me, Major," I said, "but what are you planning to do with us?"

"Monsieur Blaye," he said, "I am a soldier and I obey orders. My instructions are to accompany you and your secretary to Budapest as soon as possible, to see you safely to the Russian embassy. Judging by what Otto tells me of your condition, I do not think you will find it burdensome to travel tomorrow morning. We will catch the morning train."

"What's this all about?" I said. "And why do you continue to call me Monsieur Blaye?"

Major Strakhov smiled. "I don't think there's any doubt of your identity. First of all, Monsieur Blaye, there is your passport. Then there are the labels in your clothing and the signature on your traveler's checks." In my desire to do a thorough job I'd even signed the checks with that name. "And there is the baggage which you and Mademoiselle Torres left aboard the train."

He crossed the room to fill my empty glass.

"Monsieur Blaye, as I've already explained, I only know my orders. I was sent to Hegyshalom to meet you and to escort you to Budapest. When the sergeant of the train guard radioed ahead that you had vanished, I naturally called Budapest for instructions. I was commanded to find you and to bring you to that city. That is all I know, please."

I told the major I would very much like to get to bed. He called Otto and Hermann to carry me, but I found I could walk with Otto's arm supporting me. The major led the way to a bedroom, wished me a pleasant good night, and bowed himself out the door.

Well, I'd started out to play the role of Marcel Blaye when I thought the name was a passport forger's dream. Now that I knew that the passport was real I was stuck with the part. At least, I was stuck with it until I had to face the Countess Orlovska or someone else in Budapest who'd known the genuine Marcel Blaye.

I had been so sure that Marcel Blaye was dead. Now there was nothing certain. Had the man Maria called Dr. Schmidt murdered him in, Vienna? It could be that his body hadn't yet been found or that an alarm had not reached the Hungarian frontier station. Or maybe he was still alive, waiting for a new passport in Vienna before proceeding to Budapest?

Who was Marcel Blaye, anyway? The passport said he was a thirty-five-year-old Swiss from Geneva, a man whose description almost exactly matched mine. Maria Torres, his secretary, said he called himself a watch and clock exporter but otherwise she didn't know much about him. He was supposed to have been on his way to Budapest to close a big deal with the Hungarian government, but who ever heard of a government so hard up for watches and clocks that it sent Russian majors in full uniform to meet salesmen at frontiers? And to track them down when they jumped off trains?

I got out of bed and pulled aside the curtains. Even if I'd had my clothes and my strength, even if I'd been willing to leave Maria, there wasn't the slightest chance of escape. The windows were solidly barred. Otto and his friends weren't asleep. The major had said his orders were to find us and take us to Budapest. He looked like just the man to do it.

Of course. That was it. They thought that Blaye had decided to back out, to welsh on the deal at the last minute. They would reason that was why he'd left the train. It sounded less and less like watches and clocks. And they—whoever they were—weren't having any backing out from Monsieur Blaye.

As long as I was going to have to play the part a little longer, there was nothing to do but to tell Maria. No matter what she'd think, I'd have to give her the whole story about the passport. She was in just as much trouble as I. She had a right to know what was going on, if only for her own safety. Otherwise, I couldn't risk what she might say or do when she heard Major Strakhov address me as Monsieur Blaye in the morning.

I didn't dare turn on the light. I tiptoed to the door, expecting to find it locked from the outside, but it opened.

The corridor was dark, but there was light showing under the door of the room next to mine. I raised my hand to knock and stopped in mid-air. I had no way of knowing whether Maria or Major Strakhov was in that room. I decided to knock anyway. If the major answered, I'd ask for an aspirin.

I knocked and there was no answer. I knocked again and nothing happened. I knocked a third time and then I heard Maria's voice say, "Who is it? What do you want?" so I opened the door, walked in, and shut it and said, "It's me, John Stodder. I've got to talk to you."

I could see I'd wakened her from a sound sleep. When she'd rubbed her eyes and propped herself up in bed on one elbow, she took a look at me and started to laugh.

"What's so funny?" I said. "Let me in on it. I need a laugh at this point."

"Nothing," she said, "except you're the first man I ever met who came calling in a blanket." I hadn't realized I was still wearing the blanket that Otto had wrapped around me when he'd removed my clothes. My bare legs and feet were showing, I needed a shave, and my hair was matted like a hermit's.

I didn't know how to begin so I told her about Major Strakhov and how he had taken me for Marcel Blaye.

"You do look a lot like Monsieur Blaye," Maria said. "I told you so when I first saw you in the compartment. You fooled me when your back was turned. But I don't understand why Major Strakhov should think you're Monsieur Blaye. I can't imagine that he'd know anything about Monsieur."

"Look," I said. "It's much simpler than that." It wasn't easy to say. I must have fumbled for words. "You see, I'm traveling on Marcel Blaye's passport."

I expected her to scream or faint or point her finger at me and call me a murderer. She didn't do any of those things. She just looked at me with those big black eyes and said, "You'd better tell me the whole story."

"Well," I blurted out, "I told you my reasons for wanting to come to Hungary. I tried to get a visa on my American passport more than two years ago, but it never came through. I finally discovered that the Russians didn't like what I'd written about them in a book. It was one of those correspondent books about my experiences in Budapest when the war began in Europe. But I'd made up my mind to get to Hungary, visa or no visa. So when I reached Vienna, one of my friends who's still in Intelligence put me in touch with Herr Figl. He's supposed to be the smartest document forger in Europe. I paid Figl five hundred dollars, and he handed me Blaye's passport. I thought the name Marcel Blaye came out of Figl's imagination."

Maria didn't say a word. She just kept looking at me. I knew then how important it was that she believe me—more important than Major Strakhov or what might happen in Budapest or anything to do with the jam I'd led us into.

"You can't think I killed Blaye," I said. "You don't believe I had anything to do with getting the passport from him?"

It seemed an hour before she answered.

"No," she said slowly, "I believe you." Then she

smiled. "You see, if you'd killed Monsieur Blaye you'd have killed me, too. You could have killed me in the compartment on the train. You could have killed me anytime after we left the Orient or you could have left me in the brook when I fainted. You didn't have to take care of me but you did. No, I don't think you're a murderer."

"I got you into this jam in the first place," I said. "I promised I'd get you back to Vienna."

"If you'd left me on the train," Maria said, "I'm sure I wouldn't be alive. I told you Schmidt was following me."

I said we didn't have a chance of escaping from the lodge. I said we'd have to play along with Major Strakhov. We'd try to get away from him on the train to Budapest. Maybe we'd have to wait for an opportunity until we reached the city.

"I'd give a lot to know what Blaye was up to," I said. "It would make things a good deal easier."

"Why don't you look in the envelope he gave me to carry?" Maria asked. "It must have something to do with the deal or he wouldn't have been so insistent that I take it."

"Where is it?" I asked.

"Otto has it," the girl said. "He took it from me out there when they found us."

"I can't go wandering around," I said, "looking for an envelope. Maybe there'll be a chance in the morning. What do you think is in it?"

"I don't know," Maria said, "but I'm sure that's why Doctor Schmidt is following me. Monsieur made me promise in Vienna, before he left me, that I would keep the envelope with me. It has to have something to do with all this."

"Look," I said, "once we get to Budapest, I'll leave you. I'll put you on the first plane or train for Vienna or maybe you can go straight back to Geneva."

Maria didn't say a word. She put out her hand and drew my face down to hers and kissed me.

Chapter Four
UNWELCOME ESCORT

Our baggage was neatly stacked at one end of the platform when we arrived at the Hungarian frontier station the next morning. It had been carefully removed from the Orient and even more carefully searched. The job had been skillfully done, and we'd never have known except that the snooper had neglected to wash his hands and the odor of garlic was on everything.

The baggage wasn't the only surprise that awaited us. The local from Vienna for Budapest was ready to leave as soon as its passengers satisfied passport examiners, customs guards, money control officials, health inspectors, and the MVD. There was a note for Marcel Blaye from Countess Orlovska. And to make it a really gala occasion, there was Herr Doktor Wolfgang Schmidt promenading the platform, as big as life and twice as ugly.

Otto had driven us to Hegyshalom in the Russian staff car, over the same rutted road we had walked the night before, through the gate in the high wire fence, and across the railway tracks. Major Strakhov pointed out, in a strictly impersonal way of course, that we had

been extremely lucky to fall into the hands of Otto
and his friends. I had miscalculated our position when
we jumped from the Orient. I had remembered the
border as it was before the war. It had been easy
enough for me to sound off about friendly farmers to
drive us to Vienna. But there were no farmers for miles;
the Red Army had cleaned them out of the border
zone. And the frontier was three miles behind us when
we left the express; we were well into Hungary. If we
had eluded Otto and then escaped death from expo-
sure, we should have faced a frontier solid with barbed
wire, machine-gun emplacements, searchlight towers,
and sentries with police dogs.

Our clothes had been returned to us, neatly
pressed by Hermann, and we had breakfasted on ham
and eggs and coffee with Major Strakhov in front of a
roaring fire. We might have been an archduke's week-
end guests instead of a Russian major's prisoners.
Strakhov entertained us with stories of his boyhood in
Leningrad, and Maria never blinked an eye when he
addressed me as Monsieur Blaye. I might have relaxed
and enjoyed myself if I hadn't pictured what would
happen when we reached Budapest, when Major
Strakhov learned from Countess Orlovska that I wasn't
Marcel Blaye.

The countess's note, produced by the stationmaster
at Hegyshalom, served only to deepen the mystery.
Maria had said Blaye seemed very much in love with
the countess who visited his Geneva office. Strakhov
had added that she was "upset" to hear that Blaye had
brought Maria—"your pretty secretary."

The note, written on heavily scented pink paper, only added to my confusion.

Darling: You have acted very foolishly. A kiss and the back of her hand at the same time. *You gave me your solemn word you would faithfully carry out our bargain.* Was the Countess Orlovska included in this strange watch-and-clock deal? With Dr. Schmidt the homicidal competitor?

"What are you laughing at?" Maria said.

"It must be love," the major said. "A charming lady, the countess."

I read the rest. *You cannot, must not have any regrets at this late date. You are gaining a very powerful friend, one on whom you may always count. Suppose some of your so-called friends do object? You know you will get nowhere on your own. I anxiously await your arrival in Budapest, my love.*

It was written in German and signed *Anna.*

When Strakhov remembered he had not telegraphed the time of our arrival to Budapest and went off to the stationmaster's office, I handed the note to Maria.

She said, "I'm sorry but I don't know German. You'll have to tell me what it says." I translated it into French, but she said it didn't mean anything to her.

"Did Blaye speak German?" I asked.

"Yes," Maria said, "especially with the countess." She added, "He also spoke German with Doctor Schmidt."

"Was the countess supposed to be in on this big deal? Did Blaye ever mention her or Doctor Schmidt in that connection?"

Maria shook her head. "I don't know. I told you I knew so very little about Monsieur Blaye's business."

"Was there any connection between the countess and Doctor Schmidt? Did you ever see them together?"

"No," Maria said. "It was just the opposite. Monsieur told me that I was to keep them apart. He said that if either arrived while the other was there I was to say he was out. He was very definite about it." She linked her arm through mine. "What do we do now?"

"Go on to Budapest," I said. "There's nothing else we can do. At least there's still no alarm out for me. I expected to find half the MVD waiting. I don't get it."

The platform was lined with Hungarian gendarmes, their spiked silver-and-black helmets glistening in the sun. The only exit from the station grounds was guarded by Russian soldiers. I had thought wildly of boarding the train and leaving through the side away from the platform, trusting to find some escape through the yards, but there was a freight on the next track, apparently shunted there to discourage passengers with such ideas.

The schedule, posted in the station, told me the local took more than five hours to reach Budapest, with twenty or more stops at village stations. Maybe something would turn up in that time. I told Maria the story of Grigori, the Sultan, and the Sultan's favorite monkey. Grigori had been condemned to life imprisonment but won a year's stay by assuring the Sultan he could teach the monkey to talk. If he succeeded, he'd go free. If he failed, he'd die by slow torture. "But you know you can't teach that monkey to talk," said his wife. "I know, I know," was Grigori's smiling answer, "but something's sure to turn up in the year. Either the Sultan will die or the monkey will die or—"

"Or you will die," said a voice behind us. Maria grabbed my arm. It was Major Strakhov. How long had he been listening? "Amusing story isn't it, Monsieur Blaye? I didn't realize it was known in Switzerland. It's a favorite of prisoners in our Soviet jails. I like to think it shows the fatalism of our race."

There was a first-class compartment for us, a sticker in Hungarian and Russian on the door: *Reserved for the Embassy of the USSR.* As soon as we had racked our baggage, Strakhov handed me Marcel Blaye's passport and the traveler's checks which Otto had lifted the night before. He returned to Maria her Swiss passport and the Manila envelope she had so carefully carried from the Orient. The red wax seals were intact. The major had no reason to withhold our papers, now that he was sure we couldn't escape the rendezvous in Budapest.

From then on it was a cat and mouse game between Strakhov and me. I had to examine the contents of the envelope; Maria had passed it to me. I had to know something, anything, about Marcel Blaye's game if we were to have a chance with Countess Orlovska and the Russians in Budapest. But I couldn't rip open the envelope, supposed to belong to me as Marcel Blaye, certainly not in front of Strakhov. He might wonder at Blaye's consuming curiosity regarding his own property. And the major had made it very plain by his actions that he intended to keep me in his sight, that he was with me solely for the purpose of seeing me to Budapest.

Maria and I, with the major close by, were standing in the corridor when the station bell rang for the train to start. That was the moment for Maria to spot Dr. Schmidt on the platform.

"I beg your pardon?" said Strakhov to Maria. "What did you say?"

"She was just commenting on the beauty of those farm women," I said. "The ones down there with the geese."

"Not bad," said the major, "but you should see our Russian peasants."

The doctor couldn't have been more than fifty feet away. I caught the glint of sun on gold-rimmed spectacles, a gray Homburg on the bullet head, an almost ankle-length overcoat, yellow gloves, and a cane. I took Maria's arm but there was no sign in her face of the fear she had shown the night before.

Strakhov saw Schmidt, too, but he gave his attention to the man with whom Schmidt was conversing, a tough-looking character with a great black mustache and a patch over one eye.

The major let down the window, popped his head out, and shouted in German, "Otto, I told you to get back to the lodge. Get a move on, you loafer." He turned to me. "Didn't I say those swine are just like children? Talk to strangers, anything to get out of work."

Otto acted as if he'd been caught in the jam pot. He clicked his heels, saluted in Strakhov's direction, and disappeared on the double into the station. Dr. Schmidt boarded the train just as it started to move.

What could I have done about Schmidt? I was sure he'd been discussing Maria and me with Otto but what could I have said to Strakhov? I couldn't say, "There's the man who murdered Marcel Blaye," because I was Blaye as far as the major knew or cared. I couldn't say, "Arrest that man. He's following Mademoiselle Torres to rob her or kill her," because such a statement was equally impossible of explanation. There was another side to the situation, too. As long as Strakhov was with us, we were reasonably safe from Dr. Schmidt. The little man on the platform had seemed about half my size, but I was sure he had a gun. I reproached myself for not having bought a revolver in Vienna but I had worried about being searched at the frontier and, anyway, Otto would have lifted it the night before. Strakhov had returned the passports, the traveler's checks, and the Manila envelope but he wouldn't have given me back a gun.

As soon as the train was rolling, the major settled himself in a corner, lit an evil-smelling black cigar, and poked his nose into a copy of *Pravda*. I picked up the Manila envelope, excused myself, and started out the door, but Strakhov dropped his paper and came with me. For the next two hours I tried every excuse to shake him. When I went for a drink of water he tagged along. When I expressed a desire to stand in the corridor to watch the dreary countryside, he stood beside me. When I followed the bearded conductor to ask how late we were running, Strakhov came along. I couldn't even get away from him in the men's room.

Maria had tried to pry the major loose, but he wouldn't follow *her* when she left the compartment. He must have read *Pravda* word for word at least half a dozen times when he wasn't following me up and down the corridor. Maria produced knitting from somewhere. I sat and stared out the window and grew more and more fidgety at the thought of meeting the Countess Orlovska at the station in Budapest.

We couldn't have been much more than an hour out of Budapest when Maria came back to the compartment to announce that lunch was being served in the dining car and that she was hungry. Strakhov said he didn't care much about eating. I said I thought lunch was a fine idea, so then the major quickly agreed he'd like it after all. Maria said she'd run into the steward in the corridor and had taken tickets and she gave us each one. We went through the train in single file, pushing our way through half a dozen third-class coaches, the corridors jammed with peasants on their way to market, live geese and chickens and quacking ducks under their arms, the odor of garlic and sour red wine on everything, the cars strung with red banners proclaiming: *Long live the People's Democracy.*

We were met at the door of the diner by a smiling, bowing waiter. I thought the effusive welcome somewhat unusual, even allowing for Maria's beauty, and I put it down to the fact that Strakhov was in uniform. Most porters and dining-car stewards in the Iron Curtain countries are police informers. They know enough to be polite to Russian officials if they want to keep their jobs.

The little waiter bowed us up the aisle to the end of the car.

"May I have your tickets, please, your excellencies," he said, halting in front of a table for four, already occupied by a man and a woman. "Ah, yes, Madame is here." He seated Maria with a grand flourish. "Monsieur here." He put me across from Maria. "And Excellency Major, this way, if you please." Strakhov looked as if he would choke. His eyes nearly closed under those bushy black eyebrows but he shrugged his shoulders and followed the steward down the aisle, getting a seat with his back to us. I think he failed to put up a row because he figured we couldn't leave the diner without passing him; our end of the car was coupled to the electric locomotive, and there was a Russian guard plainly visible on the platform.

At that moment I didn't care whether the others at the table spoke French or not.

"Some luck," I said to Maria. "I couldn't figure out how we were ever going to shake that guy."

Maria's black eyes flashed. "Luck, nothing," she said. "I like your nerve. When I got the tickets from the waiter, I gave him a big fat tip. I told him we were newlyweds and we wanted to be alone."

"And you're right, too," said the man who sat next to Maria—in French, but with an American accent if I'd ever heard one. "What Europe needs these days is more romance. Isn't that what Europe needs, Teensy?"

"Oui," said the woman who sat next to me. "Uh, oui."

I was so intent on getting to Marcel Blaye's Manila envelope, now that we'd escaped Strakhov for the moment, that I was hardly prepared to have two strangers butt into our conversation.

"Romance is the thing," said the man. Then he spoke American: "By the way, do you folks speak any English? I'm afraid I'm not too good at this frog talk myself."

I said I spoke English. I couldn't see any reason why a Swiss businessman shouldn't know English. I said it before I realized I was opening the way to complications while the Manila envelope was burning a hole in my pocket. Maria said she spoke some English, too. It hadn't occurred to me to ask her.

The man grinned. "I think you both speak English real good. Don't you think they speak English real good, Teensy?"

"Yes," said Teensy. "Uh, yes."

"Folks, my name is Hiram Carr—Hiram G. Carr, to be exact. I'd like you to shake hands with Mrs. Carr." Teensy had a grip like a stevedore. "Married twenty years next February, folks. More in love than ever. Hope you young folks'll be as happy as we are. Isn't that right, Teensy?"

"Uh-huh," Teensy said.

Hiram Carr reminded me of a well-groomed sparrow. He looked to be somewhere in his early fifties. His high-pitched voice came from an incredibly small body. A good foot shorter than I, Carr had a round, pink baby face. Twinkling blue eyes shone through pince-nez, the first I'd seen in years that carried a thin gold chain hooked over one ear. His sparse gray hair, parted in the middle, looked as if it might have been barbered by Teensy, an extraordinary exhibit herself. Nearly six feet tall and big all over, she must have been a good ten years younger than her husband. Her abundant yellow hair, obviously dyed, was swept on top of her square head and held more or less in place with big black hairpins. Her expressionless face might have been made of granite with a bright dab of orange rouge on each cheek.

"What's your name if I may inquire?" Hiram Carr said.

"Blaye," I said, "Marcel Blaye." Maria bit her lip.

"Morris Blaine?" Hiram said. "Why that's an American name, Blaine. We had a fellow run for president once named Blaine. Didn't make the grade, though. Isn't that so, Teensy?"

"Uh-huh," Teensy said. She seemed a good deal more interested in the scenery.

"I'm Swiss," I said. Maria dropped her fork. I looked at the Carrs and thought *They'll arrive at the Budapest station when we do. They'll see us meet the Countess Orlovska. They'll be in at the beginning of the end of this nightmare and they'll still tell the neighbors back in Ohio about the nice, carefree Swiss newlyweds they met in the train, the ones who spoke real good English.*

The waiter brought the soup, but Hiram G. Carr went right on talking.

"What's your line if I may ask, Mr. Blaine?"

I looked at Maria. "Watches and clocks," I said. "What's yours, Mr. Carr?"

"That's a good business," Hiram said. "I almost forgot all you Swiss are in clocks or cheese." He enjoyed a small chuckle. "Well now, Mr. Blaine, I'm a diplomat you might say. Oh, I'm not one of those fellows goes to tea parties in striped pants. Fact is, Mr. Blaine, I'm the agricultural man at the American legation in Budapest. Been a practical farmer all my life and my father and grandfather before me. Isn't that right, Teensy?"

"Uh-huh," said Teensy, her mouth half full of bread.

"Where you folks putting up in Budapest?" Hiram asked.

"The Bristol," I said. I knew it was the only hotel on the Corso that hadn't been destroyed in the siege.

The meat course succeeded the soup, then fruit and cheese and coffee, but Hiram Carr twittered through it all. He talked about the Hungarian wheat crop, told us how apricots are made into barack, discussed the manufacture of paprika, tokay wines, and potato brandy, and the correct way to cook a fogash. At least it kept my mind off the catastrophe impending in Budapest until I looked at my watch and saw we were within half an hour of the city. I called the waiter and had him bring me a newspaper.

"You won't mind if I attend to a little business?" I said to Hiram. "We're combining business with pleasure on this trip."

Although I could see the back of Strakhov's thin neck from where I sat, I wanted the newspaper handy in case he should come to our table. I figured I could hide the contents of Marcel Blaye's Manila envelope by quickly folding over the paper.

I held the newspaper in front of me with my left hand, broke the seals, and slit open the envelope with the table knife. I lifted out a thick wad of typewritten sheets and placed them on the unfolded newspaper. At that moment, Strakhov left the dining car.

My hands were trembling, and I couldn't have lifted a glass of water to my lips without spilling it; but Maria was telling the Carrs about life in Geneva, and nobody seemed to notice my nervousness. I knew there had to be some vital information in that envelope, some clue to the mess we were in, something that would give me a defensive weapon in dealing with Countess Orlovska. I don't know just what I expected to find. But I wasn't prepared for what was on the typewritten sheets in front of me. Names and addresses in alphabetical order:

Ablon Jeno, Vaci utca 13, Budapest, watchmaker.
Balogh Henrik, Kossuth Lajos utca, Kecskemet,
    pharmacist.
Kovacs Pal, Kiraly Karoly utca 388, Budapest,
    garage.

And so on through the alphabet. There were more than one hundred names with addresses scattered throughout Hungary. And heading each page was the German word for watchmaker.

I don't know how long I sat there with my chin in my hands, staring at those lists, trying to make something out of them. I returned to reality when Maria nudged me.

"The waiter says they're closing the dining car. I think we'd better get back."

I replaced the lists and wrapped the envelope in the newspaper and followed Maria, Teensy, and Hiram G. Carr down the aisle and through the third-class coaches. There was no sign of Herr Doktor Schmidt.

Hiram Carr turned to me just before we reached our compartment. I was glad he wasn't going to see the sticker, *Reserved for the Embassy of the USSR,* on our door, although our fate would certainly be known to every Budapest diplomat the next day.

"Now don't you young folks go and forget us. It's been a real pleasure. The name is Hiram Carr—Hiram G. Carr to be exact—and you'll always find me at the American legation. You say you're stopping at the Bristol? Well, you'll get a ring from us real soon. We'd like to have you two lovebirds take pot luck with us. Isn't that right, Teensy?"

"Uh-huh," said Teensy.

When Maria and I reached our compartment the door was closed. I took her by the arm and walked up the corridor.

"It's no use," I said. "There's nothing in that damned envelope except the addresses of a lot of watchmakers, pharmacists, and garagekeepers. There couldn't be another envelope? Are you sure you got the right one?"

Maria said, "That's the right envelope. It's the only one Monsieur Blaye gave me."

I bent down and kissed her. "I've really gotten you

into something this time. When we arrive, just let me handle everything. Don't say a word. I don't think they'll have anything against you." I thought maybe I ought to tell my troubles to Hiram Carr. He might have helped at the American legation. But, after my story in the dining car, there wasn't any way for me to prove I was American. And there wasn't any time. We were already running through the outer suburbs of Budapest.

I slid open the door of our compartment and stood aside to let Maria enter. I thought it curious that the light was off and the shades pulled down but I supposed Strakhov was taking a nap. It was time to wake him.

I put out my hand and switched on the overhead light. Strakhov was in the corner, his hands folded on his lap and his eyes closed. The compartment looked as if a cyclone had hit it. Our baggage had been pulled off the racks and our belongings were scattered all over the seats and the floor. If the major wanted to examine our baggage, he might have done a neater job.

I put my hand on Strakhov's shoulder to wake him.

Maria would have screamed if I hadn't clapped my hand over her mouth. Strakhov's body was still warm, but there wasn't any doubt he'd never be any deader. There was a knife with a handle a foot long in his back.

I moved faster than I'd ever moved in my life.

"Stuff those things into the bags," I told Maria. I had to make her act before she became hysterical. "It doesn't make any difference how. Just clean up the place and hurry."

I picked Strakhov up under the shoulders and

dumped him on the floor, under the window. I tried to pull out the knife, why I'll never know, but it wouldn't come. I tried the seat cushions and they lifted and there was space enough to cram the Russian's body.

By the time I'd replaced the cushions, Maria had finished the baggage. I threw the bags back up on the racks. There was a bright red stain on the cushion where Strakhov had been, but I covered it with pages of the Budapest newspaper. There wasn't any hope of hiding things indefinitely. I only thought we might gain enough time to leave the train and the station before the train crew caught on.

We heard the conductor in the corridor shouting "Kelenfold, Kelenfold," and the engineer started braking for that suburban station, the last stop before the train crosses the Danube for the main Keleti station in Pest.

I grabbed a suitcase and handed a smaller one to Maria and followed her up the corridor. Then I remembered the envelope. I went into the last compartment, which was vacant, and stuffed Marcel Blaye's typewritten lists behind the cushions of the seat, wrapped in the newspaper.

We had no difficulty leaving the train. The guard had left the car platform, and there were a good many people getting off with us.

We walked down the station platform and handed in our ticket stubs from the day before to the station-master at the gate. He never noticed the difference. We were the last passengers through, and the station plaza was deserted when we came out.

My nerves were on edge, and the only thing I could think of to say to Maria was, "You know, Strakhov got that story about Grigori all wrong."

"What do you mean?" Maria said.

"Strakhov had the wrong ending. It isn't 'or you will die' at all. It's 'or I will die.'"

There was a car parked on the far side of the plaza. I thought it might be a cab. I told Maria to wait while I went over to it.

I had gone about ten feet when a figure came out of the station door behind me. It was Dr. Schmidt and he had a gun in his hand. The gun was pointed at my head.

Chapter Five
CAPTURE

It had snowed steadily all day and now at dusk it had turned bitter cold again. It was hard moving underfoot, and the few trucks and busses churned and skidded in the unswept streets. The first stars had come out in the sky, and the wind had fallen to a whisper. Thin columns of wood smoke hung suspended like exclamation points atop chimney pots on a thousand glistening roofs. The one redeeming feature of the weather was that the snow served as decent covering to the dreary ruins of Buda, the hilly half of the city on the right bank of the frozen Danube. The flickering shadows from the street lamps gave grotesque substance to the endless miles of blackened walls, and for an evening Budapest was whole again. For a bare half hour, the time required by Herr Doktor Schmidt to conduct us to the center of the city, I saw Budapest almost as I had left it a few weeks before Pearl Harbor, almost as it had been before German and Russian armies hammered it to rubble.

I wasn't surprised to find Otto and Hermann, the pants presser, waiting for Dr. Schmidt in the late Major Strakhov's staff car. They had evidently started for

Budapest on Schmidt's orders the minute our train left Hegyshalom; it hadn't required much effort to beat the local. They were wearing Russian uniforms when the doctor marched us up to the car.

Schmidt had wasted no time getting us into the car. "I must warn you not to make any trouble," he said in German. It was the first time I had heard his voice. It was clipped, hard, and precise. "I am an excellent shot. If you will be so kind, please pick up your baggage and proceed to the car."

Although Maria had told me she understood no German, she picked up the bags and came over to where I was standing. There was no sign of emotion in her dark face, none of the terror she had shown when she told me about Schmidt aboard the Orient Express. She had been close to hysterics just because he was on the same train. Now he was facing her with a gun in his hand, and she appeared calm. The only indication of what she could have been feeling was in the tightened lines around her lovely mouth. I suddenly realized how little I knew about her.

Schmidt put me in the front seat with Otto, who behaved as if he'd never seen me before. The doctor and Hermann, with drawn revolvers, sat in back with Maria between them. We drove straight to the Danube, then followed it north, past the winged victory monument of the Russians on Gellert Hill, over the Erzsebet bridge into Pest, and out the broad Rakoczi ut. We passed a dozen traffic policemen, close enough for me to have touched them, but I knew better than to call for help. Even if they had dared inspect a Red Army car, they wouldn't have believed any story I could tell them. And if they had intervened, the alternative to Dr. Schmidt was the Countess Orlovska—with the murder of Major Ivan Strakhov to explain in addition to that of Marcel Blaye.

For a time I thought Schmidt was taking us into the country. We continued out Thokoly ut, past the Park Club, and over the railway tracks, but Otto made a skidding left turn into Mexikoi ut which parallels the railroad. The street bounds one of the worst slum districts of Budapest with tenements hard against slaughterhouses, oil refineries, and fertilizer factories, the whole area a rabbit warren for criminals, a sort of unofficial sanctuary for the hunted from Istanbul to Berlin.

Otto turned into an alleyway between two dingy tenements, drove fifty feet or so, and swung the car into a junk-littered yard enclosed in a high board fence. He'd driven from Kelenfold without a word from Schmidt; he had covered the route before. I recalled Major Strakhov's contemptuous dismissal of Otto and his fellow mercenaries. "Just like children." The Russian had seen Otto talking to Schmidt on the Hegyshalom platform and he'd put it down to Otto's desire "to get out of work." If Strakhov had been a little less superior, he would have suspected that something was up and he might have preserved his own existence.

Hermann jumped out of the car and knocked on the battered wooden door of the tenement.

"Schnell," said Schmidt when there was no answer. "Hurry up." Otto hit the car horn. "Stop it, you fool," said Schmidt. "Do you want to tell the whole neighborhood?"

Hermann beat on the door with the butt of his revolver. A window on the third floor was raised, and the head of an old woman appeared, framed in the flickering light from an oil lamp.

"Wie heissen Sie?" screamed the old woman.

"Mein Gott," said Dr. Schmidt. "The old fool has lost her mind."

"You've lost your mind, old fool," Hermann shouted.

"Nein, nein," screamed Schmidt, leaping out of the car and landing in the snow up to his knees. "Dumkopf." He shoved Hermann, then cupped his hands and shouted to the woman in the window. "Open this door immediately. It is I who command. Do you hear me?"

There was a moment's silence, then the sound of the window closing, and the light disappeared. Dr. Schmidt went to the door and when it opened an inch he grabbed it with both hands and swung it back on its hinges so that it smashed against the building. The old woman was standing in the doorway with the oil lamp in her hand.

"You knew I was coming," Schmidt said, waving his finger under her nose. "Why weren't you at the door? What do you mean keeping me waiting? What is the matter with you?"

"Bitte, Verzeihung, Excellenz," the old woman said. "Please forgive me. One does not know these days. There have been police raids in the neighborhood. I thought, Excellency, I—"

"Shut up," Schmidt said. "You are not here to think."

He called to Otto. "Get those two in here immediately."

I managed to beat Otto out of the car to help Maria down. Her hand brushed my face as I swung her into the snow, and I thought she held my arm longer than necessary, but it might have been to steady herself. There was just enough light for me to see her dark face. The wide-set black eyes were calm, the firm line of her jaw was clearer than ever.

The old woman stood inside the door as Maria and I entered. I took her for well over eighty. She was thin as a skeleton, her eyes sunken and dull, her pinched face streaked with dirt. Her bony arm trembled with the weight of the oil lamp which threw long dancing shadows into the barren hallway.

Schmidt ordered the woman to lead the way, and we followed her in single file up three flights of narrow, rickety stairs at her wheezing pace, a step at a time and with only the lamp in her shaking hand for illumination. The building must have been abandoned for years. The rooms and the hallways were piled high with junk, most of the windows were broken, the walls were running damp.

When we reached the top floor, the old woman led the strange parade to the front of the house, into a room crammed with boxes and barrels and old newspapers. The slanting roof cut the height of the room so that I had to lower my head to enter. There were two dormer windows, and through the broken, grimy panes we could see the lights of the Danube Corso and the long beams of the Russian antiaircraft searchlights in the Varosliget, the city park a few blocks away.

There was a broken-down armoire, covered with dust, against the wall, on the side of the building away from the alley. The door, its glass front shattered, hung drunkenly from one rusted hinge. When the old woman had recovered her breath from the climb, she kicked the door open and stuck her head inside. When she stepped back, we could see that the back panel of the armoire had slid aside; there was an entrance to the warehouse next door.

Schmidt elbowed the old woman aside and squeezed his squat body through the armoire. A few moments later the narrow opening was flooded with light, then Schmidt reappeared.

"Hermann."

"Ja wohl, Excellenz." The pants presser clicked his heels.

"I shall need Otto here with me to help entertain our friends. But I want that car moved from here immediately. It is much too dangerous. You will drive it to Felix in Matyasfold, Verstehen Sie?"

"Ja wohl, Excellenz."

"You will give your uniform to Felix. He will return your civilian clothes and the necessary documents. He will also give you clothes and documents for Otto. You will return here promptly in one hour. If you are stopped by police, you will tell them you are Frau Hoffmeyer's nephew."

"God forbid," said the old woman.

"Shut up," said Schmidt. "You will say you are to visit Frau Hoffmeyer. Your papers will bear you out. Do you understand, Hermann?"

"Ja wohl, Excellenz."

"As soon as we are inside, you will help Frau Hoffmeyer replace the dust on this armoire and you will pile some junk in front of the door. Verstehen Sie, Hermann?"

"Ja wohl, Excellenz."

"Gut," said Schmidt. "Gehen Sie schnell." He raised his hand with the palm outstretched. "Heil Hitler."

Hermann clicked his heels for the tenth time. "Heil Hitler."

The old woman cackled. "In my day we said, 'Hoch der Kaiser.' "

"Shut up, old fool," Schmidt said. "Who cares about your day? Your day is gone forever."

Otto herded Maria and me into the warehouse room, and the armoire panel closed behind us.

The room into which we moved I took to be the repair shop for the warehouse. There were wooden benches against the three outer walls of yellow brick and without windows. The benches were cluttered with tools of every description from screwdrivers to power lathes. The fourth wall, opposite the entrance, was of rough, unpainted wood and also windowless. At one time there must have been a stairway from the floor of the warehouse, some forty feet below, but there existed no sign of it. The only ventilation came from a big skylight under which was stretched a blackout curtain on wires. The room was lighted by electricity, and in one corner there was a tank with water taps.

There was a desk against the wooden wall, opposite the entrance, and half a dozen chairs in front of it, but the main exhibit was a life-size oil painting on the wall behind the desk. The picture was lighted the way people light pictures of their more prosperous ancestors. The subject was Adolf Hitler.

"Sit down, please," Dr. Schmidt said. He placed his hat and coat and cane on the workbench, then seated himself at the desk. He might have been preparing to instruct a class in manual training except for the revolver he placed within reach. Otto stood behind Maria and me.

The doctor cleared his throat.

"I am quite sure there is no need for me to introduce myself." His tiny pig eyes gleamed behind the gold-rimmed spectacles. "Fraulein Torres I have had the pleasure of meeting in Geneva. You, mein Herr, I do not know—yet. But I shall know you very well. Is it not so, Otto?"

"Ja wohl, Excellenz."

I found myself saying to Maria, "I thought you told me you didn't understand German?"

"I don't," Maria said. Her composure made my own nerves twice as jumpy.

"I beg your pardon, Mademoiselle," Schmidt said. "I had forgotten. We shall speak French. Or rather, should I say, I shall speak French." He had the habit of cocking his head and pulling on his ear as if to emphasize his point. "I promise you shall have your chance to talk later."

Otto giggled.

Schmidt picked up the revolver and sighted it over our heads at an imaginary target. He put down the revolver, removed his spectacles, and wiped them with a handkerchief.

"First of all, you will please put Monsieur Blaye's Manila envelope on the desk."

When neither Maria nor I moved, the doctor said, "Come, come," and pulled at his ear. When nothing happened then, he said, "I'm afraid I shall have to ask Otto to find which of you is carrying it."

With Schmidt pointing the gun at me, I had to let Otto search me. I didn't like his running his hands over Maria and I must have shown it in my face because the doctor said, "Please remain calm, Monsieur."

Otto put Blaye's passport and the traveler's checks and Maria's passport on the desk. He stepped back, and we sat down.

"You examined the suitcases they took off the train, Otto?"

"Yes, Excellency."

"And what did you find?"

"A toothbrush, three odd stockings, a suit of lady's underwear, one shoe—"

"That will do, Otto. You did not find a large Manila envelope, the one you took from Mademoiselle Torres in the snow last night, the one you gave Strakhov like the fool you are?"

"There was no envelope at all, Excellency."

Schmidt picked up the revolver and ran his hand along the barrel. Through the skylight came the sound of a locomotive whistling for the grade crossing in front of the warehouse.

By this time my nerves were ragged. The whole performance had turned into a never-ending nightmare. I had come to Hungary on what I thought was a forged passport, on a personal mission, an attempt to trace my brother. I had good reason to fear the Russians and the Hungarians, the masters in this country. There was no reason whatever to get mixed up with Herr Doktor Wolfgang Schmidt, a German who sat under a portrait of Adolf Hitler in a Budapest warehouse. Whatever his racket, he was just as much afoul of the authorities as I was. A good deal more, because he'd murdered a Russian officer. The killer could only have been Schmidt looking for that damned envelope.

"Look," I said. "I don't know what this is all about and I'm not interested. If you're worried about that list of watchmakers, I hid it on the train."

Schmidt leaned across the desk. The ugly dueling scar stood out on his cheek.

"So." He picked up the revolver by the barrel and smashed the butt on the desk. "You take me for a fool. You want me to believe you left that envelope on the train? Ah, no, Monsieur, you will have to tell a better story than that."

"It's true," I said.

Schmidt said, "You will find we have ways of getting the facts."

Otto giggled.

"All in due time, Otto, all in due time," the doctor said.

He stared at me a minute or so. "I must confess, Monsieur, that up to now I had a certain admiration for you. I put you down as a clever man. Frankly, I did not suspect your existence until I saw you with Mademoiselle Torres on the Orient Express."

"There wasn't any reason for you to know about me," I said. "I'd never heard of you, either."

Dr. Schmidt laughed. "I suggest you dispense with the comedy."

I told you my nerves were ragged. I blurted out the story of my brother, the story I'd told Maria the night before in the snow, out under the stars. I told why the Russians refused me a Hungarian visa for my American passport and how I'd purchased what I thought was a forgery from Herr Figl in Vienna.

"How amusing," Schmidt said. "You do have a talent for storytelling. But you cannot suppose I am fool enough to believe such a fabrication."

He removed his glasses once more and wiped them.

"Just so that we understand each other, Monsieur, let me tell you what you've been up to. Ah, yes, I think it is all very clear."

He pounded his fat fist on the desk. "Six weeks ago, Monsieur, you succeeded in planting Mademoiselle Torres in Marcel Blaye's Geneva office."

"That's a lie," Maria said. "I never saw him in my life before yesterday."

It was the first time she'd spoken to Schmidt, but all he said was, "Please watch your language.

"I'm sure Mademoiselle Torres must have learned a great deal in that office," the doctor continued. "You see, Blaye was a fool as well as a traitor. I told him Mademoiselle Torres's father had been a Spanish Communist."

"He wasn't any more a Communist than you are," Maria said. She was sitting on the edge of her chair.

Schmidt didn't answer. He didn't even bother to look at her.

"I do not know whether you followed Blaye and Mademoiselle Torres to Vienna," Schmidt continued. "At any rate, you were there when they arrived. I must admit I thought I was rather clever in disposing of the late Monsieur Blaye. I do not hide the fact that I killed him. He was a traitor and he deserved to die. But I think now that I should have taken his passport before you found him."

"You're letting your imagination run away with you," I said. I thought how fitting it was for Schmidt to invent such a story in front of the portrait of the Fuehrer, the biggest liar of all time. "I tell you I never saw Marcel Blaye, dead or alive. I bought that passport from Herr Figl."

The doctor pretended he hadn't heard me. "Along with the passport, you took Blaye's reservation for the Orient Express and you stole his traveler's checks. Mademoiselle Torres already possessed the Manila envelope. It was very clever of you to leave Vienna immediately for Budapest. You almost succeeded in covering your tracks by jumping off the train. You might have escaped me, you might have returned to Vienna, if Otto hadn't found you."

Otto clicked his heels.

"Monsieur, I don't know who you are. You say you're American. You speak German like a Berliner and

French like a Frenchman. I don't know who you're working for but I shall find out."

The doctor's voice had begun to rise. He came around the desk and stood a foot or two in front of me. His little pig eyes glittered behind the thick lenses.

"You are going to tell me what you did with that envelope."

"I told you," I said. "I hid it on the train."

"Who did you give it to?"

"Nobody," I said. "I've told you the truth."

"Monsieur." By this time Schmidt's voice was out of control. "You are going to tell me what you did with that envelope, or shall I turn you over to Otto?"

There wasn't anything for me to say.

"There are several ways I can make you tell," the doctor said. "How would you like me to hand you over to the Russian secret police? I think they'd like to see you at 60 Stalin ut."

"That wouldn't be very smart on your part," I said. "From what I gather, the Russians are very much interested in Blaye's envelope, too. You might have a time explaining your own presence in Hungary. Otto and Hermann are deserters from the Red Army. They've stolen an army car. And what do you suppose the Russian commander would think to find you sitting under a portrait of Adolf Hitler?"

Schmidt picked up the revolver from the desk. "We can always arrange to turn you over to the Russians dead."

"That wouldn't get you your envelope," I said.

Chapter Six
HAND IN THE DARK

Schmidt was silent a moment. Then he said, in what he must have thought an offhand manner, "Where did you leave that envelope in the train?"

I shook my head. "There's a lot more to talk about before I tell you. Anyway, you don't believe I left it there."

The doctor turned to Otto. "How long will it take to make him talk?"

"Bitte, Excellenz, a few minutes, perhaps." Otto stared at me, a wide grin on his ugly face. "An hour at the most, Excellency." He pointed to the tools on the workbenches.

"You wouldn't dare," Maria said. "He's telling the truth. He did leave the envelope on the train."

"Don't worry," I said. "I haven't anything to hide. Besides, it would take Otto a lot longer than an hour to break me down." I said to Schmidt, "How do you know you've got an hour, anyway? Suppose you put this goon to work on me. How do you know you've even a few minutes to spare?"

"What do you mean?" Schmidt said.

"You know the police have already found Strakhov's

body. They must have found it when the porters went through the train. They'd pick up the newspapers, they'd see the blood on the cushions. How long do you suppose it would be before they decided to search the whole train?"

Schmidt pulled on his ear.

"Even if the police don't look for the envelope," I said, "those international trains are always cleaned before they're sent back to Vienna. Somebody is bound to find the envelope if you don't hurry."

"How do I know you're not lying?" the doctor said.

I looked at Maria and I thought I saw encouragement in her lovely eyes. "You don't know I'm not lying," I said to Schmidt, "but you want that envelope and you haven't much time to waste. You're in a hurry. You've got to take a chance. You've got to get the envelope before the Russians get it."

"I still think you handed it to someone on the train," the doctor said. "What do you think, Otto?"

It was plain enough what Otto thought and what he wanted. "Please, Excellency, let me get the truth." He hadn't liked being called a goon. He took a couple of steps toward me.

"Listen," I said. "It would be easy enough for me to say I gave it to someone on the train. I could invent a name. But you'd find out it wasn't true. And the Russians would beat you to it."

"Why are you suddenly so anxious to help?" Schmidt said. "Could it be that you don't fancy being entertained by Otto?"

"I wouldn't like it much," I said. "Not under these

circumstances. But I think I could handle him if you'd throw your guns away."

"Excellency, please," Otto said. The grin had disappeared.

I looked at my watch. "That train has been in the Keleti station more than half an hour. If the Russians haven't found the envelope, the cleaning women will."

Schmidt went behind the desk and stood looking at the Fuehrer's portrait.

"Look," I said. "I've told you a dozen times I'm not interested in your game. Neither is Mademoiselle Torres. You know why I've come to Hungary and you know why she's here. I want to start looking for my brother. Mademoiselle Torres is anxious to get back to Geneva. We don't want to get mixed up with the Russians any more than you do. The quicker you get your envelope, the quicker we'll all get straightened out."

"Suppose I send you to the railway yards with Otto?" Schmidt said. He was thinking out loud. "How do I know it isn't a trap?"

"What kind of trap could it be?" I said. "You know the Russians and the Hungarians are looking for me and Mademoiselle Torres. I'm taking the biggest risk."

"Hermann should return any minute," the doctor said. "I could send Hermann and Otto to search the train."

"You could," I said, "but they wouldn't know where to look. How long do you think it would take them to search a twelve-car train?"

"If I sent them both with you, you couldn't get away," Schmidt said. "You could be back in an hour."

"Not here," I said. "That isn't part of the plan. The moment you get that envelope, Mademoiselle Torres and I part company with you then and there."

The doctor pounded the desk again with the butt of his revolver.

"I'm the one who gives orders here."

"Okay," I said. I'd gone too far not to gamble the rest of the way. "Just as you say." I held my watch in front of my eyes. "But you're losing valuable time."

The doctor pulled at his ear. He said, "All right, but if either of you tries to trick me, I'll kill you both."

We went out just as we had entered except that Otto wore the civilian clothes Hermann had brought him. Schmidt and the two goons saluted the Fuehrer's portrait and muttered, "Heil Hitler," as they passed through the sliding panel in the armoire. I managed to get behind Maria going down the stairs but I didn't dare speak for fear Schmidt might change his mind. Our only slim chance lay in leaving his hideout. But I had no illusions about his ultimate plan for us. Whether or not we found Marcel Blaye's envelope for him, Maria and I were scheduled to die. We knew far too much.

The old woman led us down the rickety stairs in single file with the smoking oil lamp in her shaking hand. She didn't utter a sound, but amazement was written deep in her wizened face; it could have been the first time any of the doctor's guests had left the place alive.

Hermann had exchanged the Russian staff car for a small black sedan. Schmidt told him to drive us to the

Keleti station, but Hermann shook his head. "They've blocked off the station, Excellency. There must be a hundred men with tommy guns." Hermann grinned at me. It was the first time I'd noticed his bright red hair.

When we came out of the Mexikoi ut onto the main avenue, we could see the lights of the police cars where a roadblock had been set up in the direction of the station. Hermann plunged into the side streets to make a wide detour and approach the railway yards from the south. It had begun to snow again and it was hard going through the narrow curving alleys that skirted the Kerepesitemetö, the municipal cemetery two short blocks from the station.

Schmidt commanded Hermann to stop the car in front of a small coffeehouse, opposite the gates of the cemetery.

"Mademoiselle Torres and I will wait inside," the doctor said. "See that you return quickly."

He wasn't going to risk prowling through the railway yards with Otto, Hermann, and me. Maria was to be the hostage. Schmidt knew I'd come back to the coffeehouse for her if I came out of the yards alive.

I started off without a word, but Maria grabbed my arm.

"I'm going with you," she said. "I can't let you go alone."

I didn't trust my reactions at that point so I found myself saying, "What good could you do?" There was pain in her deep black eyes. "I'm sorry. I didn't mean it that way. You stay here with Schmidt. We won't be more than half an hour. Then we'll be free."

Before I could stop her, she put her arms around my neck and kissed me. It didn't look as if we'd just met twenty-four hours earlier. I knew it would reinforce the doctor's belief in his own version of our association.

We were turning the corner when Schmidt opened the door of the coffeehouse and we heard the sobbing of the gypsy violins.

There's a Romany tale that up in the moon,
Each midnight a gypsy is playing a tune.
The melodies sweet from his fiddle that flow,
Are heard only by lovers as silent they go.
Then, my love, let us try while the moonlight is clear,
Amid the dark forest that fiddle to hear.

There wasn't much light except for the flickering gas lamps on the street corners, and because of the drifted snow it was difficult to tell where the sidewalk ended and the street began. When we reached the main avenue which parallels the yards we found we were well below the roadblock. There was no one in sight.

We crossed the avenue, wading through snow above our knees. There was an iron fence beyond the far sidewalk. On the other side of the fence were the dark and silent trains under a mantle of white.

Otto stood aside and motioned to me to climb the waist-high fence.

"Don't be a fool," I said. "There may be a sentry." There was a space between the fence and the first line of coaches and it looked recently swept. "We'll wait five minutes." Otto, who didn't like me at all, started to say something, but he and Hermann were so accustomed to authority that they followed me to a billboard which screened us from the tracks.

It was five minutes before the sentry plodded past us on the other side of the fence, then another three minutes before he returned. I timed him carefully because a knowledge of his position would be handy when the time came to leave the yards.

As soon as the sentry was again out of sight, we went behind the billboard. Otto indicated that I was to go first. Thereafter I led the way. I would draw first fire if we were surprised. And, should I attempt a getaway, they had a clear line of fire without the risk of hitting each other. I didn't like the way Otto kept his hand on his gun in his pocket although I felt sure they wouldn't shoot until we had found Marcel Blaye's envelope.

I hadn't much idea how I'd identify the right train when I saw it but I remembered the photographs of Innsbruck and Salzburg in our compartment so I looked for the *O.B.B.* marking of the Austrian State Railways—the Oesterreichische Bundesbahnen. The only cars on the first siding were third-class Hungarian coaches.

Snow had drifted under the cars, and it would have been much easier to have climbed into a car vestibule and to have gone out the other side, but the doors were locked, and we crawled on our hands and knees under the couplings.

I think we were at the fifth or sixth track from the street, making escape from the yards almost impossible if we were surprised in force, when Hermann spotted an Austrian car. We moved to the head of the train and there was a blue Wagons-Lits diner, still carrying the plaque: *Wien-Gyor-Budapest*. We were far enough out in the yards so that there was some light from the arcs.

Hermann boosted me onto the coupling at the head end of the diner, and I pulled myself into the open vestibule. I tried the door into the car, and it was unlocked. We had no flashlight. I used my lighter until the wick burned out. Then we took turns lighting matches.

Visit the Riviera, said the ads in the dining car. *Sunshine All Year 'Round. King David Hotel, Jerusalem—American Bar. Hungary Welcomes You to Her Ancient Festivals.*

It was colder in that train than outside. Our footsteps echoed down the empty corridors. Doors opened and shut with a crash that shook the windows.

We went through half a dozen third-class coaches before we reached the car in which Strakhov, Maria, and I had traveled. The coaches hadn't been cleaned, another reason for us to hurry. The train was scheduled for early-morning departure for Vienna; the cleaning crews were due any minute.

I looked for the sticker on the door of our compartment—*Reserved for the Embassy of the USSR*—but there was none. I thought I'd made a mistake and went to the next car back; there was no sticker there either.

I imagined the police had detached the coach the moment Strakhov's corpse had been found. Maybe the car was on another siding, for the photographers and the fingerprint experts of the MVD.

I went through the two first-class cars again, looking for a compartment with framed photographs of Salz-

burg and Innsbruck, but that didn't help. All compartments had pictures of Salzburg and Innsbruck.

Otto and Hermann followed me up and down those
cars without a word. When I closed the door in the last
compartment, I became aware that Otto had taken his
revolver from his pocket. Hermann stood behind Otto,
peering at me over his shoulder.

"What's the game?" Otto said. "What are you trying
to put over?"

"I'm not trying to put anything over," I said. "I can't
find the right compartment. Keep your shirt on."

I led them to the head compartment in the first car
but there was no envelope stuffed behind the seat
cushions. I saw that Hermann, too, had his revolver in
his hand.

"It's in the other car," I said. "It's in the head compartment in the other car." But the envelope wasn't
there, either.

"I'll give you two minutes," Otto said.

"There's something very wrong," I said. I had to stall
those two killers. "I know," I said. "They must have
backed the train into the station. They've changed the
position of the diner for the run back to Vienna. I've
been looking in the wrong compartments."

I didn't believe it though; I walked as slowly as I
could. It came to me that Schmidt never had any
intention of letting me leave the train alive. Otto's instructions were to murder me in that train, whether or
not we found the envelope.

I thought I heard a door bang. Maybe it was the
cleaning crew.

"What's that?" I said.

"Nothing," Otto said. "Nothing but your imagination. It seems to have been working overtime. So you did hand that envelope to someone after all?"

There was nothing behind the cushions in the compartment in the first car.

"I'm freezing to death," Hermann said. "What are we waiting for, Otto?"

"He's got another minute," Otto said. It was too dark to see their faces.

"The hell with another minute," Hermann said. "It's warm in that coffeehouse and there's plenty to eat and drink."

I kept on walking, into the second car and down the corridor, the two Germans' footsteps echoing mine. By that time we'd run out of matches, but it made no difference. They could pump me full of bullets in that narrow corridor without aiming.

I took as much time as I could to slide back the door in that last compartment. The metal handle was burning cold through my glove. Otto stood just back from the doorway as I went in. The compartment was as black as the inside of your pocket.

I fumbled along one end of the compartment but there was nothing behind the cushions. I thought of attempting to escape out the window, but Otto would hear me. He'd kill me before I could lower the sash.

I turned and leaned over the seats on the other side. Maybe Otto wouldn't squeeze the trigger until he'd examined the envelope. If I found it. *If.*

My mouth was dry, and I was shivering with the cold. I was sure Otto could hear my chattering teeth.

I felt in the corner but there was nothing behind the cushions.

I edged toward the center. There still was only empty space where an envelope wrapped in a newspaper should have been.

I put out my left arm to search the corner. But my hand never reached the corner.

Someone grabbed my wrist. I tried to shout but I had no voice. I crashed to the floor with the explosion.

Chapter Seven
RESCUE FOR A PRICE

For a split second I thought it was Otto who had fired. Then Otto's body pitched through the doorway to land on the floor on top of me. Whoever had seized my wrist out of the dark had fired.

The explosion was deafening. It was a few seconds before I made out a voice saying quietly, "Get on your feet. Get on your feet and open the window. Hurry." It was a vaguely familiar voice, speaking English.

I started to my feet, and my hand touched Otto's face. I said, "Be careful. There's another one out there." I felt someone brush past me, then a shot crashed down the corridor. I stood stock-still. There was no outcry, there was no answering shot.

I pulled down the window. The wind felt good in my face.

"Get out," said the voice behind me. "Get out. We haven't any time."

I landed in the snow. There was enough light flickering through the falling snow so that I caught the gun that dropped from the window. It was Otto's Luger.

Sound came on the wind from the station. There were three quick shots, warning shots fired into the air. There were shrill blasts from a whistle.

I turned back to the window to see a body drop out.

It landed in the snow alongside me. It was a woman, a six-foot, broad-shouldered woman with bright yellow hair. I helped her to her feet. It was Teensy, the taciturn amazon from the dining car, the wife of Hiram Carr, the American agricultural attaché. She wore ski pants and heavy boots and a short jacket with a fur collar. Her head was bare, and the two bright spots of orange rouge were still on her cheeks. There was also a .45 in her hand.

"Get going," she said. She emphasized her words with a shove. "Crawl under the cars, get to the fence. Above the billboard. Hiram's there with a car. Get going."

I ran toward the head of the train through the drifted snow. I ran toward the lighted part of the yards because the billboard was opposite the second car. I had no choice. Men were coming from the opposite direction, from the station. I could see the dancing beams from their flashlights as they ran.

I ran like a frightened rabbit, but Teensy got to the fence ahead of me. She was in the car, holding open the door, when I scaled the fence. I jumped into the moving car.

Teensy sat in the front seat with Hiram who drove. He was dressed like something out of Fenimore Cooper and Sears Roebuck combined, blue overalls tucked into the kind of boots farmers wear in the cattle barn, a navy pea jacket, and a coonskin cap, complete with tail. Teensy lit me a cigarette.

When we'd driven a good mile, Hiram turned his head and said in his high-pitched voice, "Well, well,

Mr. Blaine, such a genuine pleasure to see you again. Isn't that so, Teensy?"

"Cut the comedy," Teensy said. "If I have to hear any more of your folksy patter I'll get out and walk." She turned to me, "Mr. Stodder, Hiram thinks he has to pretend to be a hick just because he's supposed to be an agricultural attaché." I've had to listen to the same low-comedy act all over Central Europe. 'Don't you think they speak English real good, Teensy? Been a practical farmer all my life and my father and grandfather before me.' He's never been any closer to a farm than Times Square. His father kept a saloon in Brooklyn. I don't think he knows who his grandfather was."

Hiram laughed. "It's surprising how many people take you for just what you pretend to be." Then he added mischievously, "Isn't that so, Teensy?"

"You're an idiot," Teensy said but she leaned over to kiss him on the cheek.

"Look," I said. "Would you mind letting me out anywhere here? I've got to get the girl who was on the train with me."

"Where did you leave her?" Hiram said.

"In a coffeehouse," I said. "About two blocks from the station, across from the cemetery. She stayed there with Schmidt while I went into the yards."

Instead of stopping, Hiram stepped on the accelerator.

"Where are you going?" I said. "It's in the other direction." I thought of using the Luger in my pocket.

"Don't worry," Hiram said. "We'll go with you. We won't leave Mademoiselle Torres. But I've got to get rid of this car. We may have been spotted."

It didn't seem strange that Carr should have known Maria's name. Or that Teensy should have addressed me as Stodder. Not after everything else that had happened to me in twenty-four hours.

We drove ten minutes in silence. Then Hiram drove into a gas station, parked the car, and handed the keys to the attendant. We piled into another car which carried diplomatic license plates. Several pairs of skis were strapped to the top.

"We've been skiing in the Buda hills," Hiram said. "Keep your mouth shut if we're stopped."

I felt a lot better when I saw Schmidt's car in front of the coffeehouse. I said I thought Hermann must have joined the doctor and Maria when he left the yards.

"What are we going to do?" I said. "We can't start a gun battle in there with Schmidt."

"Never mind about that," Hiram said. "Schmidt doesn't want trouble any more than we do." He stepped out of the car. "You'd better stay out here. It's close enough to the station so that some of the train crew might be inside. They might recognize you. There might be police."

Teensy said, "Get behind the wheel and keep the engine running. You'd better be sure that gun is working."

I lowered the window. I looked at my watch, and it was a few minutes before nine o'clock. Maria had been inside with Schmidt nearly an hour and a half.

Apparently the apricot brandy was flowing freely; when Hiram opened the coffeehouse door the patrons were singing with the gypsy band. Hiram and Teensy couldn't have been gone more than five minutes but it seemed to me they'd never return. Two or three times I swore with impatience and found myself opening the door to follow them. Teensy had left me a pack of cigarettes; I smoked one after another. If I inspected the safety catch on that Luger once, I looked at it twenty times. A policeman passed, swinging his nightstick. He must have heard the engine because he stopped and stared at the car. I took the gun in my hand when he came close. But he looked at the diplomatic license plates, turned on his heel, and walked away.

Teensy came out of the coffeehouse first. She said, "I'm afraid there's a hitch."

"What do you mean?" I said. I didn't like the look in her face.

"Your girl isn't there," Teensy said. "The proprietor said she and Schmidt left an hour ago."

"You couldn't have looked for them," I said. "She wouldn't have left. Schmidt wouldn't have left his car here. You didn't look far enough. The proprietor's a liar."

Teensy shook her head. "We looked all right. They've been gone nearly an hour, the proprietor says."

Then Schmidt couldn't have been alerted by Hermann. The doctor hadn't waited for Hermann or anybody else. He never had the intention of waiting. He'd ordered Otto to kill me in the train, whether or not we found the envelope.

But how could Schmidt have forced Maria to leave a public place against her will? He couldn't have used a gun unless the proprietor and all the patrons were in league with him. It didn't make sense. I remembered my doubts about whether Maria understood German. I recalled contrasting her calm in Schmidt's hideout with the stark terror she'd shown at the mere sight of him on the Orient Express. Why had she—

Hiram's high-pitched voice brought me back to earth. "If you'll slide over, we'll get moving."

"Where are we going?" I said. "What about Schmidt and the girl?"

Hiram let in the clutch. "You're coming to our place. There's a lot you're going to tell me. Then we can think about how to find Mademoiselle Torres. And put that gun in the glove compartment. You'd better unload it. You won't need it now."

Hiram drove to the Danube, then headed north along the quais.

"Have you ever been to Budapest before?" Teensy asked.

I told her I'd lived there for more than two years, from the beginning of 1939 to just before Pearl Harbor. But I had something else on my mind.

"Will you let me keep the Luger?" I said to Hiram.

"No," he said. "You still want to leave us?"

"Yes," I said. "I've got to know what's happened to Maria, to Mademoiselle Torres. If you'll let me out anywhere along here."

"Nothing doing," Hiram said. "We aren't running a rescue business for free. I want information from you and I want it right away. Besides, how far do you think you'd get without us? You'd be picked up in an hour by the police. Do you understand Hungarian?"

I said I did. Hiram switched on the car radio.

The announcer was saying, "The People's Democracy has brought peace and prosperity to Hungary."

"What's that got to do with anything?" I said.

"Wait a minute," Hiram said. "Just be patient."

There was a lot more of the usual Communist party-line harangue, then the "Internationale."

"Attention," the announcer said. "The Ministry of the Interior has issued the following communiqué:

"A reward of 25,000 forints will be paid for information leading to the arrest of foreign agents, guilty of murdering a Red Army officer on Hungarian soil. The crime was committed this afternoon aboard the Vienna-Budapest local train by a man and woman, traveling on Swiss passports made out in the names of Maria Torres and Marcel Blaye. The Capitalist perpetrators of this unspeakable act are believed to be in the neighborhood of Budapest, having escaped from the train at Kelenfold station before their crime was discovered. All citizens are ordered to telephone police headquarters or notify the nearest policeman the moment this dangerous pair is spotted. Warning: they are believed to be heavily armed."

Hiram switched off the radio. "They've been broadcasting every fifteen minutes. Do you want us to let you off?"

"I've got to do something about the girl," I said. "I won't leave her."

"We want to see her just as much as you do," Teensy said, "but not for the same reasons."

Hiram seemed to find the remark very humorous.

"And I'd like a long talk with Herr Doktor Schmidt,"

Hiram added. "Take my word for it, Mr. Stodder, Schmidt won't kill her. He won't do anything until he knows where that Manila envelope has gone."

I said to Teensy, "Then you found it?"

"No," she said. "Somebody must have been ahead of us."

"How did you know about the envelope?" I said.

"It's a long story," Hiram said. "I'll explain when we get to our place. But I saw you were very anxious to examine an envelope in the dining car. Then Teensy saw you duck into the end compartment on your way out of the train. We figured you went in there for a purpose. But we didn't get a chance to look before the train arrived at Keleti. They sealed the car after they found the Russian's body."

We passed the Franz Josef bridge, and the Russians' winged victory monument was black against a blacker sky over the Gellert Hill. We passed the Elizabeth bridge, and there were the naked walls of the royal palace atop the Buda hills.

The Carrs lived in a big, old-fashioned house at the end of the Stalin ut, near the City Park. The house was less than a mile in a straight line across the park from Schmidt's hideout on the Mexikoi ut.

The door was opened by a smiling man whom Teensy addressed as Walter. She said Walter and his wife Millie, who did the cooking, had been with the Carrs for many years. Walter was an ex-prizefighter, a heavyweight. I'm over six feet, but Walter towered over me.

Hiram produced a shaker full of cocktails but

neither he nor Teensy would discuss Maria or Schmidt or Hungary until we'd finished Millie's chicken dinner. Hiram said they hadn't been back to America in more than five years and he quizzed me on everything from major league baseball to the old age pension. After dinner, after he'd poured the Benedictine and thrown a couple of logs on the open fire, we talked about what was on our minds.

I told my story for the third time, just as I'd related it to Maria the night before, the way I'd told it to Schmidt, the story of my brother and how I'd bought Marcel Blaye's passport for a forgery. Twenty-four hours earlier, even three hours earlier, it had sounded reasonable and logical. With each later telling, it began to assume a quality of fantasy until it sounded only half real to me. I found myself wondering whether I hadn't suffered some sort of mental aberration and that perhaps neither Maria nor Schmidt nor Strakhov nor any of them had ever existed.

I told the Carrs everything, step by step, until Teensy found me in the dark and silent train in the Keleti yards. She and Hiram listened without moving except to throw logs on the fire from time to time or mix me a highball.

"And that's all I know," I said. "How do you two fit into all this?"

Hiram lit a cigar.

"The night before last," Hiram said, "I was called on the telephone from Vienna. I was told to get over there right away. There wasn't a train or a plane so Walter drove us over."

He paused to look at Teensy, but his remarks were still addressed to me. "You mustn't expect me to tell you everything," Hiram said. "But since you've been frank with me, I'll tell you all I can about the mess you're in.

"When we reached Vienna, we were told that a man named Marcel Blaye, in whom a great many governments had expressed interest, had been murdered. Fortunately, if one can use that word in connection with murder, Blaye's body was found in the American zone. I say it was fortunate because public knowledge of his death would be most inconvenient at this time. Doctor Schmidt knows Blaye has been murdered because he killed him. But the Russians still do not know Blaye's fate. All they know is that an envelope which he was carrying was brought into Hungary by Mademoiselle Torres, his secretary. They know that Major Strakhov accompanied someone with Blaye's passport on today's train. They still think it was Blaye himself. I propose they go on thinking so."

Hiram's feet just touched the rug when he sat on the edge of the leather armchair. The cigar was almost as big as the smoker.

"One of our men from Vienna was on the Orient Express. He was following Doctor Schmidt just as Schmidt was trailing Mademoiselle Torres. Unfortunately, our man was not sufficiently imaginative to foresee that you would leave the train. In the first place, he did not know of Blaye's passport. All he knew was that you had purchased the space which Blaye's death had made vacant. Unlike Doctor Schmidt, he proceeded to Budapest and wired Vienna in code from the legation. That's why Teensy and I took this morning's train."

"How do you know I'm not mixed up with the Russians?"

Hiram blew an enormous smoke ring. "In that case, you wouldn't have found it necessary to leave either the Orient or today's train."

Teensy said, "We thought at first you might be French or British, until I met you in the yards."

"I'm eternally grateful for that," I said. "I thought I was finished. Both of those goons were ready to shoot me."

Hiram smiled. "My wife is a quick thinker when she has to be."

Teensy stuck out her tongue at him.

"But usually we find our team works better when I do the planning and Teensy does the legwork. I think I should be a ridiculous object in a rough-and-tumble shooting match. On the other hand, Teensy is quite capable of taking good care of herself."

"Look," I said. "What is this all about, anyway? Maria told me Blaye was a watch and clock exporter. She told me about his office in Geneva and how he said he was coming to Budapest for a big deal with the Hungarian government. What the hell goes on?"

"It's a long story," Hiram said, "but I'll tell you what I know about it since we're in the same boat."

"What do you mean, the same boat?" I said. "I appreciate everything you've done for me and I've told you everything I can. I want to get Maria out of

Schmidt's hands and send her back to Geneva. Then
I'm going to look for my brother. That's the only reason
I came to Budapest."

Hiram shook his head. "I told you we weren't running a rescue business for free and I meant it. Whether
you like it or not, you're going to see this thing through
with us."

"And supposing I refuse?"

"You won't," Hiram said. There was a hard quality
to his voice I hadn't heard before. "You're an American
and you'll stick with us. But, even if you hadn't made
such a decision on your own, I think we've ways to influence you. We could turn you over to the Russians
or Doctor Schmidt. Or we could send you to Vienna to
be executed by a firing squad for the murder of Blaye.

"You see, Mr. Stodder, you've gotten yourself mixed
up in a very serious business. This is a matter of life
and death for nations as well as individuals. You've
taken a hand in a game that could influence the issue
of war or peace in Europe and the world."

Chapter Eight
UNWILLING ACCOMPLICE

At that moment, Hiram's pronouncement didn't impress me in the slightest.

"But that doesn't help me find Maria," I said. "I'm not going to leave her in Schmidt's hands, no matter what your problem is."

Hiram was very patient. "Nobody said you had to. I told you I want to talk to her and I've got some questions for Schmidt, too. You'd better make up your mind right now that there's nothing you can do to rescue Mademoiselle Torres without our help. All I'm asking is that you realize finding her is also part of my problem."

"What's this problem?" I asked. "What's this threat to the peace of Europe and the world? And what do you mean by 'peace' anyway? Who said there was any peace in the world? I'm one of the thirteen million Americans who fought for peace. I haven't seen anything that looks like peace."

"All right, then," Hiram said. "There isn't any peace. But there still isn't a shooting war. At least, *we* aren't in one. Perhaps I ought to say that the outcome of this little problem might mean the difference between America's winning or losing a shooting war."

"Go ahead," I said. "I'm listening."

Hiram asked Teensy to fill our glasses.

"The whole thing goes back to the Fall of 1944," Hiram said. "At least, this phase of it does. In one way or another it's been going on for a century."

I suppose I was fed up because I had to sit there and listen to Carr talk in what I considered silly generalities instead of going to Mexikoi ut to get Maria.

"Please skip the preliminaries," I said. Both Hiram and Teensy looked at me. "I'm sorry. I guess my nerves aren't what they ought to be."

"I don't blame you," Hiram said. "I'll try to be as brief as possible.

"Let's start in 1944, in the fall. By October it was evident to everyone, except probably Adolf Hitler, that Nazi Germany was finished, that it was impossible to continue resistance against Britain and the United States in the west and Russia in the east.

"A little over a month later, French troops would be fighting the Germans in the streets of Strasbourg for possession of the city itself. But already the Nazis knew what it meant to have the blitzkrieg, their own invention, turned against them. The Allies were fighting on the sacred soil of the Reich itself, something Hitler had boasted could never happen. The Siegfried Line had been cracked in the west, and in the east the Russians were attacking Hungary, the last ally left to Germany in Europe.

"On the tenth of October, 1944, there was a meeting at the Rotes Haus, the famous old hotel in Strasbourg which was still in German hands. That meeting was attended by the nine leaders of the nine basic industries of Germany.

"We had a man working at the Rotes Haus as a relief waiter. He'd been in Strasbourg before the war and had been parachuted back. He managed to send us a good many details by radio before the Nazis caught him. As a waiter, he served the nine Germans and learned a good deal of what was going on."

"Who were they?" I said.

"The names aren't of any interest now," Hiram said, "even if I could remember them. They were, of course, outwardly Nazi like everybody else of importance under Hitler. But they were really the representatives of the Junkers and the Ruhr industrialists, the men who, generation after generation, are behind the governments of Germany, whether those governments are headed by Hitlers or Kaiser Wilhelms or Konrad Adenauers. You follow me?"

"Yes," I said. "They're the men who look upon 1914-1918 and 1939-1945 as just a couple of battles in a long war. I remember talking with a German diplomat who thought that way, even in the summer of 1939."

Hiram and Teensy waited for me to continue. I guess Hiram figured I'd be easier to handle if I became enthusiastic.

"It was right here in Budapest," I said. "It was the German minister. He was a member of the Prussian aristocracy who had served in the German diplomatic service for twenty years before Hitler took over. He told everybody he abhorred the Nazi regime but he served it faithfully."

"What were you doing here, Mr. Stodder?" Teensy asked.

"I was a newspaper correspondent," I said. "The Hungarian press chief invited me and two Hungarian editors to dine with the minister. I didn't like the Nazis, but my business was to get news and I went.

"Anyway, it was the evening that Berlin and Moscow announced the famous ten-year treaty between Germany and Russia. I asked the German minister what he thought would follow. He said he thought war was inevitable. Then I asked him what he thought would be the outcome of such a war. He said he felt Germany would lose."

"He must have been drinking," Hiram said. "Most of them weren't that frank."

"Oh, he'd been drinking, but the payoff was his next statement. He said that he thought Germany would lose but she would win the next one, the Third World War."

"What was his reasoning?" Teensy asked.

"He said Germany would lose but it would only be a token defeat. Just as in 1918, he said, Britain and France would be terribly weakened. He said Germany, no matter what happened, possessed greater powers of recovery. He felt Britain and France would be dying nations even in apparent victory."

"What did he say about Russia?" Hiram asked.

"He said that, pact or no pact, Germany and Russia would fight each other. But I remember what he said after that just as clearly as if it were yesterday.

"The German minister said something like this:

'Russia may fight alongside Britain and France. She might help swing the coming war against Germany. But Russia is Asiatic. Russians are ruthless. You would soon find Russia would try to rule Europe. England would eventually fight Russia as England has fought every nation that has tried to dominate Europe. Then our chance would come. Germany would pick up the pieces.' "

"That fits in with my story," Hiram said. "It all fits perfectly.

"Those nine men who met at Strasbourg also looked at the Second World War as a battle in what they regard as another Hundred Years' War, one they fanatically believe will end in German victory in spite of two lost battles. Because they regarded the second battle as lost, they met to send German industry underground. They couldn't send all of their industry, of course, but they could send the key scientists, the men responsible for so many of Germany's military weapons. They would continue to work in secret on their inventions against the day when a new German army would be ready."

I drained my glass. "A lot of people in America are talking about rearming Germany today," I said. "You hear arguments that Western Germany ought to be allowed a certain number of infantry divisions. You hear a lot of talk like that in Washington. They think they can use the Germans against the Russians."

Hiram nodded. "Your German minister was certainly right. The Russians have already armed the 'people's police' in Eastern Germany. But nobody will benefit except the Junkers and the Ruhr industrialists.

"Early in 1945, the plan to send the German war scientists underground was put into effect. Some of them were instructed to surrender to the British and the Americans as refugees. Others went into the Russian lines. A good many technicians went to Scandinavia and Switzerland, others to Spain and Portugal. You see, it didn't make any difference in the long run where they continued their work as long as they were ready to return to Germany when the time came. They were to continue their scientific research anywhere they could, even to pretending to work for the Russians, the Americans, or the British. They would have facilities at their disposal and they would also form a sort of scientific intelligence corps, learning other countries' secrets at the same time."

It was a further development of the old scheme for keeping their soldiers in training, even to noncoms like Otto and Hermann who had joined the Red Army as frontier guards. A new version of the Trojan Horse.

"Do you think Germany was about to produce new weapons when the war ended?" I asked. "If you remember, Hitler kept promising the Nazis marvelous new weapons if they would hang on a few months longer. Everybody was talking about the neue Waffen. Do you believe it was only propaganda?"

Hiram lit another cigar. "No, I know it wasn't all bluff on Hitler's part. There's a lot of evidence to show they'd made tremendous new advances in rockets, for instance. But they never got into production."

"Haven't all those things been outdated by the atom bomb and the hydrogen bomb?" I asked.

"Certainly not," Hiram said. "Suppose the Germans invented a controlled rocket which would travel 10,000 miles, one that could carry an A-bomb or an H-bomb? There's good reason to believe they did."

I said, "I don't quite see what this has to do with Marcel Blaye and why he was killed by Doctor Schmidt."

"I'm coming to that. There was a gap of many months between the time we were tipped off by the relief waiter in Strasbourg and the occupation of all of Germany. Even then the Russians had gotten into Berlin before the British and Americans and the Reds had first crack at what was left of Nazi records. It took months and years of patient intelligence operations to pick up any trail. The nine German industrialists and their Junker associates had planned very thoroughly." We could hear the screaming siren of a police car moving down Stalin ut. It reminded me that we were only two blocks from number 60, the headquarters of the MVD.

Hiram said, "Almost every line we followed ended at a blank wall. Then, a couple of months ago, we turned up Marcel Blaye in Geneva. As Mademoiselle Torres told you, Blaye had arrived in Geneva early in 1945. He had set himself up in business as a watch and clock exporter which gave him all the excuse in the world to travel and to carry on an extensive correspondence abroad. Blaye was a German. His real name was Count Manfred Blomberg. His grandfather had been Swiss and so he was able to get a Swiss passport. Blaye, or Blomberg, was a contact man between some of the exiled underground scientists and his principals who remained in Germany."

"Who is Schmidt?" I asked.

"As far as we know," Hiram said, "a former colonel in the Wehrmacht. I don't know whether you've ever heard of a group of ex-generals and staff officers in Germany who call themselves Die Bruderschaft, the brotherhood? That's the outfit that is plugging for the rearmament of Western Germany. They're behind the campaign to sell the United States and Britain on allowing Western Germany a few infantry divisions.

"Of course, the brotherhood is tied up with the industrialists and the Junkers."

I recalled Maria's story of the angry scene between Blaye and Schmidt in the former's Geneva office. "What did Schmidt have against Blaye? Why did he want to kill him if they were members of the same gang?"

Hiram poured us another drink, then stirred the fire. Teensy was sound asleep on the sofa.

"I told you we found Blaye in Geneva a couple of months ago. The Russians had beaten us to it. By the time we became interested in Blaye, they'd sent the Countess Orlovska, one of their best agents, to work on him. And she succeeded, too."

I still had the pink perfumed note in my pocket. I handed it to Hiram.

"Then the countess talked Blaye into making a deal with the Russians?" I said. "She mentions Blaye's solemn word in regard to a bargain."

"That must have been it all right," Hiram said. "The countess is an extremely attractive woman. She knew how to handle Blaye. I suppose she made her favors contingent on his selling out his friends. Maybe she promised him a high place in the new East German government."

"The Manila envelope contained dozens of addresses," I said. "Addresses of watchmakers and pharmacists and machine shops. I wish I knew who has it."

"There's only one way to find out," Hiram said. "That's to go to the Countess Orlovska. We haven't got it. We know Schmidt didn't find it, unless his game is a lot more subtle than it seems. If the Russians have it, Orlovska may know where it is."

He left the armchair and stood with his back to the dying fire. He looked more than ever like a grotesque doll, with his head barely reaching the level of the mantelpiece.

"Do you recall anything about the lists?" he asked. "Can you remember any of the addresses?"

"I didn't try to memorize them," I said. "You'll recall I had no idea what they meant. Even if I'd known, I wouldn't have tried to memorize them at that point. My only thought was to get away from this business."

"Do you recall any detail at all?"

"Only the first name on the list. I remember because the name was Ablon, the name of an old Hungarian friend. I think the notation said this Ablon was a watchmaker on the Vaci utca. Does that help?"

"Maybe," Hiram said. "It might help if nothing else works. But we've got to work on the Countess Orlovska. We've got to get that list fast before the Russians start working on it."

"How do you propose doing that?"

Hiram flicked his ashes into the fire.

"That's a job for you," he said.

"Me?" I said. "What's that got to do with me?"

"Lots," Hiram said. "I think you're ideal for that job. Orlovska likes handsome young men. She's never seen or heard of you before. Your French and German are good enough so you can be French or Belgian or Austrian. Or you can just go on being Swiss."

"Thanks," I said.

"The only man who might be in a position to identify you in the circles in which Orlovska moves is Major Strakhov and he's dead."

I got up and went over to the window. "Nothing doing," I said. "I told you, Mr. Carr, that all I want is to get out of this mess. I want to send Mademoiselle Torres back to Geneva, then I want to trace my brother. I haven't the slightest further interest in the whole affair. I'm certainly not interested in Countess Orlovska."

Hiram replied as if he were talking to a recalcitrant child.

"Mr. Stodder, I think you'll do it. Do I have to repeat ad nauseam what I told you about the pressure I can apply? No, I think not. Even if you can't see your duty as an American—"

"I know all about my duty. I didn't spend four years in the Army Air Force for the cultural advantages."

"I think you can understand what refusal might mean to you, Mr. Stodder." Hiram was very patient. "Need I remind you again that you are dependent on me? Without my help, you cannot save Mademoiselle Torres. You cannot even save your own life."

"What are you planning?" I said. I didn't feel very friendly.

"I propose that you get some sleep. I'll have Walter wake you at midnight,"

"Midnight? Why midnight?"

"Because," Hiram said. "You're going to visit a few nightclubs. I think you'll run into the countess."

"How about Maria? What are you going to do about Schmidt?"

Hiram rang the bell for Walter.

"We shall visit Doctor Schmidt. But, Mr. Stodder, you don't think for one moment that he has taken Mademoiselle Torres back to the Mexikoi ut? We shall have to locate him. I already have two men on the job. You spoke of Hermann leaving the Russian staff car in Matyasfold, with a man named Felix. We shall watch Matyasfold, too."

"Why can't we go to the warehouse now?"

Hiram looked at me incredulously. "Mr. Stodder, we are enemies in an armed camp. Would you behave like the American police raiding a gambling den? We must move slowly and cautiously. We must operate here behind the Iron Curtain with our wits.

"Let me reassure you again, Mr. Stodder. Doctor Schmidt won't let any harm come to Mademoiselle Torres until he knows what has happened to the precious envelope. That's up to you to discover. Go to bed now and get some sleep."

Chapter Nine
IN THE DRAGNET

I was dog-tired, but it was a long time before sleep came.

I was Hiram Carr's prisoner, whatever he chose to call it. I might possibly escape him. There were no bars on the window, and it would have been an easy jump from the second floor into the drifted snow. But the alternatives to following Carr's orders were even less attractive.

First there was the overwhelming possibility that I'd be picked up by the Hungarians or the Russians before I'd moved very far from the house. Without a passport I was lost. If I eluded the police, I'd still have to find food and shelter. The reward offered for my capture would make denunciation certain the minute I appeared in public.

Suppose I left Carr's house after stealing a gun, then made my way safely across City Park to Schmidt's place on the Mexikoi ut? How could I get past the old woman in the tenement without alerting the doctor?

I thought of trying to flee Hungary, of making my way to Yugoslavia or Rumania on foot; I knew it was insanity to think of crossing the fortified frontier into Austria. But I had no money other than the traveler's checks which I had stupidly signed with the name of Marcel Blaye. I knew there was an anti-Russian underground in Hungary but why should I expect any help there, even if I could make contact?

Over and above such considerations, however, I wasn't ready to abandon the mission for which I'd come to Hungary. I had found it increasingly difficult to live with my feeling of guilt in regard to my brother Bob; to leave Hungary after having started my search would make life impossible. And now there was the added fact of Maria. The thought of leaving her in the custody of Schmidt after all we'd been through together didn't make sense. If she later proved to be something other than what she had pretended that would be different. For the moment, I had no choice but to stick with Hiram Carr.

It seemed to me my head had just hit the pillow when Walter shook me. After I'd shaved a two-day beard and showered, I found a dinner jacket laid out, complete to boiled shirt, studs, and a black Homburg.

Hiram was in his study, in front of the fireplace when I followed Walter downstairs.

"How do you feel?" he said.

"Not too good," I said. "I don't think your idea is too smart. What happens if the police ask for my papers?"

"I've taken care of that." He handed me a passport, another Swiss one. It gave my name as Jean Stodder, address—Geneva, profession—watch and clock exporter.

"Why didn't you try cheese this time?" I said. I had

begun to resent Hiram Carr intensely. I also noticed he'd lifted the photograph from Blaye's passport which Walter must have taken from my pocket while I was asleep.

"The watch and clock business will give you an angle," Hiram said. "Maybe you can talk to the countess about Blaye."

"Look," I said. I was plenty mad. "I consider this whole scheme of yours insane. How do I meet this woman in the first place? What excuse do I use? What makes you think her escort's going to welcome a pickup by me?"

Hiram was too smart to laugh out loud, but his blue eyes twinkled through the old-fashioned pince-nez.

"If I know anything about the Countess Anna Orlovska, she'll spot you the minute you walk in."

"Walk in where?"

"You'd better try the Arizona first, then the Moulin Rouge. She'll be in one or the other."

"Suppose I meet somebody who knows me? I told you I lived here for two years. What do I tell them?"

"Tell them politely they've got you mixed with someone else. But you won't meet anybody you know. The kind of people who hang out in Budapest nightclubs these days were slinking around back alleys in Moscow when you were here last. All the diplomats have changed and the government officials. I don't think you'll see any of the same chorus girls after nine years, even in the Arizona."

"How do I know what this female looks like? How do I identify her?"

"You can't miss her. She's tall and blond and she's always surrounded by a dozen admirers."

"Why is it," I said, "that female spies are always tall and blond? If you'd dream up a short, fat, dumpy one, she'd be easier to charm."

"But not half as much fun," Hiram said.

"What do I do after I meet her?"

"Arrange to meet her again tomorrow."

"I can't walk the streets. Do I come back here tonight?"

"I should say not. You never heard of Hiram Carr and I don't know Jean Stodder from—from John Stodder. Go to the Hotel Bristol. If you'll take the trouble to look at your passport, you'll find you arrived in Budapest by air two days ago and are stopping at the Bristol. The night man knows you well. I'll get in touch with you tomorrow."

Hiram gave me a Luger in a shoulder holster and a wad of Hungarian money. Then Walter drove me to within two blocks of the Arizona.

For years I had looked forward to returning to Budapest. I had always liked the Hungarians, their friendliness toward strangers, their carefree attitude. "Let the horse worry," the Hungarians said, "his head is bigger." The nightclubs of Budapest, its gypsy bands, its numberless little inns and restaurants and its famous coffeehouses, were unexcelled anywhere in the world. And there had been traditionally warm friendship for Americans.

But I hadn't counted on coming back to Budapest with a price on my head. The first thing I noticed when

Walter let me out of the car was a yellow poster, freshly tacked on a wooden fence:

> *25,000 Forints Reward for Information Leading to the Arrest of Foreign Agents Guilty of Murdering a Red Army hero on Hungarian Soil.*

It followed the radio announcement almost word for word, and there must have been a dozen such posters in the two short blocks to the Nagymezo utca where the nightclubs faced each other across the street.

I went into the Arizona, checked my hat and coat, and went to the bar. I hadn't been in the place for nearly ten years, but it hadn't changed. The same two-story room, open booths on raised platforms against the two side walls, the orchestra against the fourth wall opposite the entrance. The turntable dance floor was crowded with officers in uniform, men in dinner jackets, and women in evening gowns. The Arizona had been a mechanical marvel in the old days, and the gadgets still worked, for occasionally, with squeals of delight, the occupants of a booth would push the elevator button and the whole booth would disappear from sight into the cellar, to pop up again when a second button was touched.

I had scarcely time to order a drink before a slim blond girl perched on the bar stool beside me. She said her name was Ilonka and she preferred champagne. I don't suppose she could have been more than seventeen or eighteen. The orchestra was making such a din in the small room, playing "Deep in the Heart of Texas" for the cavorting Russians and Hungarians, that Ilonka had to shout. I understood her Hungarian but I shook my head. If I admitted speaking the language I'd have to acknowledge previous visits to Budapest. The girl would report our conversation to the headwaiter who informed the police on all newcomers. Ilonka would get a percentage of my bar bill; the more I drank, the more money she made and the more information she would theoretically gather for the headwaiter. She also doubled in the chorus line.

She tried halting German. "You are new in Budapest, is it not so?" The bartender poured her a glass of champagne.

I told Ilonka I'd flown in from Geneva two days before.

"Then you are Swiss?"

I said I was.

"You are an engineer, perhaps?"

"In a way," I said. "I'm in the watch and clock business." I glanced at the crowded dance floor and wondered which blonde was Anna Orlovska. "Is this place always so crowded?"

Ilonka tossed down her champagne and ordered another. I told the bartender I'd coast on my whisky.

"The Arizona is always jammed," the girl said. "It's always full of diplomats and government people. And black-market operators."

"I've heard Budapest is famous for beautiful women," I said.

"Thank you," Ilonka said. "Do you like me?"

"Of course," I said. "I think you're charming. But I

mean society women. Who are some of those women on the dance floor?"

The girl smiled and slipped her arm through mine.

"You'd better take it easy. The Russians don't like foreigners staring at their women. You're too nice to get yourself into trouble."

"I'm just curious," I said. "I wondered if there were some famous people here."

She swung around on the bar stool and nodded toward the booths. "That tall thin man is the minister of finance. That fat woman is his wife." Ilonka giggled. "Oh, sometimes officials do come here with their wives."

"Who's the blonde in the third booth?" I asked. "She's with the bearded man."

"Oh, that's Lilli Karvas. She's the star of the National Theater. You wouldn't like her. She throws things."

"Aren't there any Russians here?"

Ilonka looked at me curiously. "There aren't any Russian women," she said. "The Russians don't bring their wives and daughters to such places." She put her hand on my arm. "Are you married?"

"No," I said, "I'm not married." I looked across the dance floor. "Who's that Russian in uniform? The one who's alone in the booth."

Ilonka looked the other way "I like you," she said. "Let's dance."

When we'd left the bar, she put her mouth close to my ear. "You mustn't ask so many questions. It isn't healthy in this place."

The dance floor was jammed, and it was hard to move without getting an elbow in the back or a heel in the ankle. When we came in front of the band Ilonka said, "The Russian is Colonel Lavrentiev."

"Who's he?" I said. "He looks as if he were dressed for parade."

"He's head of the MVD," Ilonka said. "Will you please talk about the weather?"

"Does he come for the show?" I asked.

"He's in love with a Polish countess," Ilonka said. "She meets him here every night. Now mind your business or I'll leave you here on the floor."

When we were back at the bar I made up a lot of fiction about trying to sell Swiss watches and clocks to the Hungarian government. Hiram Carr hadn't briefed me but I felt I ought to tell Ilonka something she could repeat to the headwaiter. I said I was staying at the Bristol and would make my first visit to the ministry of commerce the next day.

I bought Ilonka another champagne. "You're afraid of the Russians, aren't you?" I said. There was no one within earshot. I didn't realize the place might be wired. "Is everybody afraid to talk here in Hungary?"

Ilonka frowned. I noticed how thin and frail she was. Twelve years of war and occupation represented almost her whole life.

"We're all afraid," she said simply. "My father says the evil eye has returned among us."

"The what?" I said.

"The evil eye. The Magyars fought hundreds of years

to get rid of the Turks from the east. Now, my father says, the barbarians are here again."

"Don't let them hear you," I said. "Don't you know they invented civilization?"

She pointed to a small glass object pinned to her dress. "See?"

"What's that?"

"That's the good eye." She unpinned it and handed it to me. "It protects us from the evil eye." It was made of blue glass to represent a human eye.

"You don't believe that?"

"Of course." Ilonka was surprised. "Don't Swiss people believe in the evil eye?"

I'd seen the charms in Turkey. I'd had a chauffeur named Murad who refused to drive my car without one on the radiator cap. I knew that Slovak peasants paint their huts blue to keep evil spirits away, that Polish farmers rub garlic on barn doors to keep vampires from milking their cows at night. But Budapest had been a civilized capital when I left in '41.

"I must get ready for the show," Ilonka said. She took my hand. "Promise you'll wait?"

I said I would. I'd have an excuse to sit alone at the bar until the Countess Orlovska showed up. Though I hadn't the foggiest notion what to do then.

I watched Colonel Lavrentiev's image in the back-bar mirror. He was a big, broad-shouldered man, the typical square-faced, square-headed blond Slav. Like the late Major Strakhov, Lavrentiev wore a full-dress uniform complete to epaulets and a large patch of decorations. He was the first Russian I'd seen sporting a monocle, an affectation some Red Army officers had picked up from the Prussians. Lavrentiev was apparently a two-fisted drinker. There were four bottles in front of him.

Then the show started, and I forgot Lavrentiev and Herr Doktor Schmidt, Hiram Carr, and Herr Figl, the grave-robbing Austrian, until I caught sight of one of the chorus girls who looked enough like Maria to make me catch my breath. Then the spotlight reflected a mouthful of gold teeth, but the shock was enough to make me feel guilty and highly uncomfortable, sitting in a nightclub drinking whisky when I should have been searching for Maria.

The show was something to see, just the same, the way I'd remembered it from the days before the proletariat ran the place. The prima donna came out of the wings on the back of a baby elephant, chorus girls floated around the ceiling on hidden wires, the dance floor rose ten feet in the air complete with tap dancers, the band thumped joyously through a dozen ancient American tunes. Colonel Lavrentiev clapped and laughed and beat time on the table with a whisky bottle.

I needn't have worried about identifying the Countess Orlovska. The chorus was wiggling through the finale when I saw Lavrentiev pull himself to his feet. He swept the empty bottles onto the floor, bellowed at the orchestra leader, and turned to face the entrance. The music ceased abruptly with a wail of the saxophone, the chorus line shuffled to a halt on one foot. Lavrentiev fixed his monocle, lifted his left arm in a sort of Roman-emperor gesture, and Anna, the Countess Orlovska, swept across the floor and into his booth. Neither performers nor patrons seemed surprised; if they were they knew better than to show it in front of the chief of the MVD.

It was easy enough to see Anna Orlovska's attraction for Marcel Blaye, Colonel Lavrentiev, or any other man. Her ash-blond hair, worn in a short pageboy bob, contrasted strikingly with her dark eyes and full red mouth. An off-the-shoulder white satin evening gown set off her dark skin.

If Anna Orlovska was concerned with the disappearance of Marcel Blaye or the murder of Major Strakhov she didn't show it. She smiled broadly at Lavrentiev as he bent to kiss her hand. She spoke to a couple in the next box and swallowed in one gulp the glass of champagne the colonel offered her.

The show never did pick up again after the colonel stopped it, and Ilonka was back with me in the bar in a few minutes.

"Does the colonel end the show like that every night?" I said. "It must be tiresome for the customers if the countess always enters in the middle."

"He does it every time she arrives," Ilonka said, "which is nearly every flight in the week."

She didn't smile, and when the bartender went to the other end she said, "There's something going on."

"What do you mean?"

"It looks like there's going to be trouble."

"Trouble, how?"

"The place is full of policemen."

"Cops get into nightclubs free all over the world," I said.

Ilonka shook her head. "It isn't that. There's half a dozen backstage. And the headwaiter says two carloads of gendarmes just drove up outside."

I figured she wouldn't be telling me if she'd been the one to suspect me.

"What do you think they want?"

"They must be looking for someone," Ilonka said.

The music started, and I took Ilonka to the dance floor.

I wondered how the police had learned I was at the Arizona. I was sure Walter and I hadn't been trailed from Hiram Carr's. I didn't think I'd said anything to arouse Ilonka's suspicions. Swiss travelers were certainly common enough in Budapest. I found myself scanning the faces of the dancers, but there wasn't one I could recall ever having seen before.

When the orchestra started a waltz, Lavrentiev followed Anna onto the floor. My first impulse was to retreat to the bar as fast as possible. But I realized that haste would make me conspicuous and I was sure that neither the Russian nor his partner had ever set eyes on me. Dancing was better than sitting at the bar wondering how long it would take the cops to close in on me.

I tried to keep to the opposite side of the revolving floor, away from Lavrentiev and Anna. It took a lot of maneuvering what with the constant turning of the waltz and the movement of the turntable under my feet. The colonel was remarkably agile despite his size, and I tried to change my pace as he did, anticipating the changes in the music.

I was so occupied with watching Lavrentiev and Anna that I didn't spot the sour-faced minister of finance and his fat wife until they had stepped onto the floor directly in our path. Ilonka said, "Look out," and I saw them and managed to pivot past but the movement threw us off stride, and the revolving floor did the rest.

Before I knew what was happening we had crashed squarely into the chief of the MVD and his partner, the two people in all of Hungary I least wanted to see—together.

Chapter Ten
DANGEROUS ACCIDENT

We must have made a ridiculous sight, the pompous Lavrentiev in his full-dress uniform, Anna Orlovska in a Paris gown, Ilonka, and me, all four sprawled on the moving dance floor. But if any onlooker dared laugh, I didn't hear him. I was certain the Russian would order me shot the moment he regained his feet.

Luckily, the bandleader pulled the switch, and the turntable came to a stop. I picked myself up and helped Ilonka to her feet. The kid was frightened speechless, and her make-up stood out like a neon sign against the white of her skin. I turned to the colonel and he was brushing off his medals. He made no move to help Orlovska so I put out my hand to aid her. The music had stopped dead. Out of the corner of my eye I saw the tense faces of the customers and the waiters.

The countess took my hand without glancing at me. She called me a clumsy lout in Polish and a lot of other words I'd heard in the seamier quarters of Warsaw. Her skin-tight satin gown had split in half a dozen places, and her pearl necklace had broken and spilled all over the place.

Lavrentiev, having finished brushing his epaulets,

had taken a step off the floor toward his table when Orlovska grabbed his sleeve. He had apparently drunk enough to temporarily forget his precious dignity in favor of the full bottle the waiter had just brought. But Anna Orlovska was having none of it.

"Boris, are you out of your mind?" She screamed like a fishwife and she spoke German for the benefit of the customers.

"What shall I do, Anna?"

"I have been insulted. We have both been insulted. These peasants have insulted the Fatherland."

I touched Ilonka's elbow, trying to tell her to get off the floor and let me face Orlovska's wrath but she was frozen to the spot.

"Boris, do something. Are you man or mouse?"

For all his power as chief of the secret police, Lavrentiev was firmly under Orlovska's thumb. Like the late Marcel Blaye.

The Russian colonel turned his square face to me and said, "Pig."

"Do something," Orlovska screamed. "Have them arrested. Have them punished."

Lavrentiev wasn't too drunk to realize he was the center of a spectacle that would provide Budapest with hilarious gossip for days. He'd either have to act to save his face or find some way of coping with Orlovska. He acted. He bellowed at the embarrassed headwaiter to call his orderly.

I thought it high time to open my mouth.

"It is all my fault," I said in German. I bowed to Orlovska. "I am guilty of the grossest carelessness. Believe

me, I apologize from the bottom of my heart." I turned
to Lavrentiev. "And you, sir, kindly accept my most sin-
cere apologies."

"Look at my dress," Orlovska screamed at Lavrentiev.
"My Paris gown."

"I shall be only too happy to see that Madame is pro-
vided with a new one."

Orlovska said, "Peasant," and then for the first time
she looked me in the face. She looked at me twice
before she did a classic double take. The second time
there was recognition written all over her face.

There's an ancient superstition that a man's life passes
in review when he's drowning. It could be, because I
reviewed my own life at that moment and I couldn't
dredge up any remembrance of ever having set eyes
on Anna Orlovska. The Europeski Hotel in Warsaw in
1939? Paris, Berlin, Rome? Budapest in 1941?

Orlovska couldn't have been on the Orient Express
from Vienna. Hadn't Strakhov said she'd come to Hegyshalom with him from Budapest? She hadn't seen me
on the train to Budapest, unless Strakhov had lied.

Maybe she thought me Marcel Blaye. But that was
ridiculous. Maria had known I wasn't Blaye and if Orlovska had been his mistress she wouldn't be fooled.

But there *was* recognition on her face. First disbelief,
then open-mouthed amazement. Then she started to
say something, swayed a little, and fainted dead away.
Maybe she had hurt herself when she'd first hit the
floor. Maybe that was it and my imagination was playing
tricks on me.

If I hadn't grabbed for her arm and caught it, she'd

have hit the floor again because Lavrentiev, having called his orderly, was no longer interested. He was already back at his table, pouring a drink.

Hiram Carr had sent me to the Arizona to meet Anna Orlovska. I'd accomplished that part with dispatch. There I was, standing in the middle of the dance floor, surrounded by gaping customers, waiters, and chorus girls, holding the limp body of the countess in my arms. Ilonka was standing beside me, trembling like a leaf. The befuddled Colonel Lavrentiev was tossing half a glass of whisky down his tree-trunk throat, the only unconcerned person in the joint.

I had to do something so I yelled, *"Föpincér,"* and the headwaiter wiped the glassy look from his blood-shot eyes and came running. My yell galvanized everyone into action. The whole place burst into loud conversation, the bandleader started an encore of "Deep in the Heart of Texas," the headwaiter and one of his minions relieved me of Orlovska, and Colonel Lavrentiev's orderly slapped his paw on my shoulder and propelled me toward the exit.

I managed to turn my head before we reached the door and I saw that Ilonka was right behind us. I pulled a wad of bills from my pocket and threw them to her. "Pay the bar bill," I said, "and keep what's left for yourself."

She grabbed my arm, but Lavrentiev's orderly told her to beat it.

"I'm sorry," Ilonka said. "I guess you just aren't a very good dancer."

It was a hell of a time to tell me that, but she dropped

something in my pocket, then turned on her heel and went off to the bar without looking back.

We stopped at the checkroom for my hat and coat. There was a short flight of glass steps leading to the main entrance. There were lights under the glass, and when you walked on the steps a music box was set in action. It had played the first few bars of the "Rakoczi March" when I first visited Budapest; now it sounded suspiciously like the beginning of the "Internationale."

When we went down the stairs, the orderly still clutching my shoulder, I could see on the sidewalk the gendarmes that Ilonka had mentioned. They were lined up facing the entrance, parallel to the street, as if waiting for inspection. Two big military cars were across the street. I suppose I ought to have been flattered at such an armed turnout in my honor.

I automatically started out the door to be handed over to the gendarmes, but Lavrentiev's orderly steered me into the doorkeeper's room, hard by the exit. He sat me down in a chair.

"Let's see your passport," he said.

I handed him the Jean Stodder-Geneva document. He read the statistics out loud.

"You've got plenty of nerve," he said, laughing. He threw the passport into my lap.

I could have told him I was frightened stiff. Why didn't he hand me over to the gendarmes? The Russians must have known who I was the moment I first stepped into the Arizona.

"Do you get drunk in Switzerland and knock down colonels on the dance floor?"

I could have told him I wasn't drunk, that I hadn't intended to crash into the colonel and Anna Orlovska. But there wasn't much use of saying anything. He was having his kind of fun before he sent me off to 60 Stalin ut.

"You're lucky Colonel Lavrentiev didn't pull a gun on you," the orderly said. "He's got a quick temper. He's a dignified man."

I didn't say anything. I wondered why he hadn't searched me for the gun. I was sure he could see the bulge in my coat. He must have thought I wouldn't dare try anything, not with half a hundred gendarmes with carbines a few feet away. Of course, they'd take the gun the minute he handed me over.

I think I could have snapped the gun from the shoulder holster quickly enough to beat him to the draw. But it wouldn't have done me a bit of good. The minute I fired, those gendarmes would have filled that little room and me full of lead. I think I've got as much guts as the next man, but that sort of death has never had any attraction. Anyway, I'm a follower of Grigori and his monkey.

"Well, come on, Herr Stodder," the orderly said. "It's time you were getting to bed."

This time I laughed. I knew enough about 60 Stalin ut to make his remark very funny. A lot of things would happen to me but not bed.

The orderly stuck his head out the door and called, "Jozsef, Jozsef." But instead of one of the gendarmes, the grubby doorman appeared.

"A taxi, Jozsef, for Herr Stodder." I didn't know who

the orderly thought he was kidding, me or Jozsef, but I didn't miss the wink he gave the doorman.

"I thought you'd rather leave in a taxi, Herr Stodder," the orderly said.

"Very considerate of you," I said. "I appreciate the courtesy."

Well, the doorman returned and the orderly showed me out the door and there *was* a taxi drawn up at the curb. The ranks of the gendarmes had parted to let me through. I got into the cab and moved over, but the orderly slammed the door after me, touched his cap, and said, "Hotel Bristol," to the driver.

It was my turn to faint and I damned near did. But I knew I had to get that driver to move his antique cab before Anna Orlovska had time to tell her story. He had hopped out and was spinning the crank, it was that old a car.

"Hurry up," I said. "I've got to get to the Bristol in a hurry." I spoke Hungarian and I didn't care who heard me.

I ought to have realized what had been going on. I should have known it from the minute Colonel Lavrentiev turned his back on me on the dance floor. I was being kicked out of the Arizona as a foreign drunk who had had the ill manners to upset the chief of the MVD and his partner, I was a harmless drunk as far as they were concerned. They were looking for someone in the Arizona all right. They knew I was there. But they hadn't put two and two together. What man in my position, the presumed murderer of Major Ivan Strakhov, would have the stupidity to come to the Arizona in the first place, then crash into the head of the secret police in the second?

Anna Orlovska was the only one who'd recognized me and she'd passed out before she'd had a chance to say a word. My only hope was to get that taxi out of there before she came to and blabbed to the police. Hiram Carr had sent me to meet her but he hadn't foreseen what would happen. I'd failed and now I had the right to save my own life.

"What's the matter?" I yelled to the driver. "Let's get out of here."

He was spinning the crank for all he was worth and blasting the night air with Hungarian oaths, the choicest on earth. I hopped out and got in the front seat but the ignition key was turned on. I moved the spark back and forth but still nothing happened.

There wasn't another cab in sight. The only vehicles were the two Hungarian police cars.

I went up to the captain of the gendarmes. Since I was supposed to be a drunk, I was careful to lurch appropriately. I made the Hungarian language lurch, too.

"Excellency Captain," I said. "Knowing the great and unbounded hospitality of the Hungarian people, may I ask one favor for an enchanted traveler?"

An American cop might have said, "G'wan, beat it," but the Hungarian smiled indulgently. A foreigner who takes the trouble to learn a small country's language can have almost anything he wants from the flattered natives.

"Might one of your mighty cars give this miserable cab a push?"

I watched the door of the nightclub out of the corner of my eye. I expected to see Lavrentiev or his orderly or one of the detectives emerge any minute. Orlovska couldn't stay in a faint forever. She'd put the finger on me the moment she came to. I thought of walking, but it was snowing again. I also had no intention of going to the Bristol. As soon as the taxi was out of sight of the Arizona, I would tell the driver to take me to Hiram Carr's. I'd done what he asked. It wasn't my fault I'd failed. The next move was up to him. I'd been wasting my time in a nightclub when I ought to have been looking for Maria Torres.

The captain of the gendarmes ordered one of his cars to push the cab. The taxi driver was so disgusted he threw his crank into a snowbank before he got behind the wheel. I huddled in the back seat, by this time shivering from a combination of frayed nerves and the cold.

The military car hit the back of the taxi hard enough to break our necks, then churned snow until I couldn't see through the windows. We slid and slithered, moved ahead and slipped back in convulsive jerks, the cab driver cursing at the top of his lungs, the gendarmes urging on the pushing car with alternate cheers and groans. I don't suppose any hunted man in the annals of crime ever attempted a getaway in such circumstances.

Within a few minutes we'd collected a good-sized crowd, passers-by, customers in evening dress leaving the Arizona and the Moulin Rouge across the street, just plain derelicts who were glad to forget for the moment their lack of shelter, mixed with the gendarmes and the policemen off the beat. Everyone shouted advice, the cab driver cursed and thanked each one in turn, and the driver of the gendarme car spun his wheels until his tires were smoking. But all the effort was a waste of time. Nothing but a snowplow or a derrick could have budged that taxi.

I stepped out of the cab and sank into the snow up to my waist. The crowd got a big laugh out of that, too, but they hauled me out and onto the sidewalk.

"Tough luck," one of the gendarmes said, helping me to brush the snow off my clothes.

"What are you guys doing here?" a man in a derby asked the gendarme. "Since when does the gendarmery pull taxis out of the snow?"

The gendarme laughed. "The Russians have some guy bottled up in the Arizona. They wanted to make sure he wouldn't get away." He leaned toward us. "Confidentially, it's the foreigner who murdered the Russian on the train." He pointed to the postered wall adjoining the Arizona. "You must have seen the notices. I could sure use that reward. They say he's a tough guy but I'd like to see him get past me."

"I think I'll stick around and watch," the man in the derby said.

"I wouldn't," the gendarme said. "There's apt to be a lot of shooting. Didn't you see where it says he's heavily armed?" He pulled his coat collar tighter around his throat. "Anybody's a damn fool to be out this time of night in this weather if he can stay home."

I said good night as casually as I could and started to work my way through the crowd. They'd heard about the murderer inside the Arizona. They were no longer interested in the minor drama of a foreign drunk in evening clothes and a snowbound taxicab.

I got through the crowd and started down the Nagy-mezo utca. My impulse was to run but I was afraid the gendarmes might be watching and I didn't dare look back. I must have exaggerated the lurching gait of a drunk; I'd never been more sober in my life. It was hard to force myself to go slowly, but I knew I'd give in to blind terror if I didn't.

I measured my progress toward the end of Nagy-mezo utca by the yellow posters on the walls: 25,000 *Forints Reward for Information Leading to the Arrest* —I wondered how long it would take them to dig up a photograph of me. It would be strange to see your own face staring at you from a thousand walls and fences.

I had almost reached the corner when I heard the shouts behind me.

Then I did run.

Chapter Eleven
MISTAKEN IDENTITY

I made the corner all right without a shot being fired but I ran smack into the arms of a policeman.

"What's your hurry?" he said. He clamped an enormous fist around my wrist. I couldn't have reached my gun, and he carried a .45 in a holster outside his fur-collared greatcoat.

There was no longer any shouting behind me. Maybe he hadn't heard it. Maybe he was just pounding his beat.

"I'm sorry," I said. "Pardon me." I tried to edge past him but he blocked the way.

"What's your business?" he said. "Explain yourself."

I knew as well as he that gentlemen in evening clothes don't run out of the Nagymezo utca at three o'clock in the morning. And he knew I wasn't a native because I spoke Hungarian with an accent.

"I'm cold," I said lamely. "My taxi got stuck in the snow. Ask the gendarmes if you don't believe me. I'm walking back to the Hotel Bristol. I decided to run to get warm."

He was short and squat, and his slant eyes showed his Tartar ancestry. His eyes also showed he didn't believe a word I'd said.

"Where are you coming from?" he said, although he must have known there was nothing in the Nagymezo utca except the Arizona and the Moulin Rouge.

"The Arizona," I said. "I stopped in for a drink."

"Maybe you're all right," he said, "but I think we'd better go back to the Arizona and be sure."

"I'm a guest of your country," I said. "What's wrong with running to keep warm? I'm not used to your cold weather, that's all. You've no right to treat me as a suspicious character. I don't think your superiors would understand such behavior on your part."

Then he wasn't so sure. Perhaps I was a Russian. Hungarian public servants who crossed the Russians usually regretted it. After all why risk trouble? Even if I had done something wrong, he could always deny having seen me.

He shifted uncertainly from foot to foot and then the argument became strictly academic because a third person rounded the corner from the Nagymezo utca and joined our little group.

It was Anna Orlovska, wrapped from head to foot in sables. The cop, who knew quality when he saw it, clicked his heels and saluted. Hungarian Communists click their heels and salute the aristocrats, even when they're nabbing them for the hangman.

"Thank you, Officer," Orlovska said sweetly. She called the cop *Rendör bacsi*, which means Uncle Policeman. Hungarian children call policemen Uncle.

"Your Highness," the policeman said. He wasn't going to make another mistake. If the lady was the wife

or the mistress of a commissar, so much the better.
"Your Highness, may I be of service?"

I expected half a dozen gendarmes to follow Orlovska
around the corner at any moment.

"You have been of service, Uncle Policeman," Orlovska said sweetly. "You have done me a great service
in detaining this gentleman."

All the countess had to do was to point to the yellow
poster on the wall behind us. Twenty years of walking
a beat at night, arbitrating Mrs. Kovacs's disputes with
her drunken husband, chasing sneak thieves and threatening suspicious gypsies was about to end. The arrest of
a public enemy of such magnitude, the murderer of a
Russian major, the stealer of the soon-to-be-famous
Manila envelope, would mean a promotion to the rank
of sergeant, a raise in pay, a medal, perhaps even nom-
ination as Hero of the People's Democracy.

Perhaps Uncle Policeman had a premonition of the
fame which was about to be thrust upon him. At any
rate, he moved his revolver from the holster.

"You won't need your gun," the countess said. Then
some of her friends *were* around the corner. I couldn't
imagine why she hadn't called them. I had to admit
she'd had a lot of courage to turn that corner alone,
whatever her obscure purpose. She couldn't have
known the policeman was there. Or was it part of
the general deployment aimed at my capture? Maybe
they'd deliberately let me out of the Nagymezo utca.
They didn't want to risk a gun battle in the Arizona?

"You see, Uncle Policeman," Orlovska said, "this

gentleman ran away from me in the Arizona. We're old friends. If you hadn't stopped him, I wouldn't have known where to find him."

The revolver went back into the holster; the cop clicked his heels again and saluted. Orlovska gave him a broad smile, slipped her arm through mine, and said, "And now, Uncle Policeman, if you'll be so kind, please tell my chauffeur to bring the car. He's just around the corner."

I followed Orlovska into the car. By this time I wasn't sure whether such things were really happening to me or whether I'd lost my mind. Until I found the answer I was determined to keep my mouth shut. The longer I stayed away from the police or the MVD, the greater chance I'd have to make a getaway.

I expected Orlovska to tell the chauffeur, "Sixty Stalin ut," but she told him to drive home. In a few minutes we crossed the Danube, climbed the Rose Hill through devastated Buda, and headed for the higher hills to the west. There was a roadblock at the beginning of open country, but the gendarmery captain waved the driver on although half a dozen cars had been halted and lined up at the side of the road.

Neither Orlovska nor the chauffeur had any comment. There wasn't a word spoken until we turned off the highway onto a gravel road and the car had stopped under a porte-cochere. Then, when Orlovska and I had gotten out, the countess told the driver to return to Budapest.

"See that Colonel Lavrentiev gets to his apartment," Orlovska said. "Tell his orderly to fill him with aspirin."

She opened the door with a key, then switched on the lights. We were in a long hallway, apparently running the depth of the house, with a stairway in the far right corner. There was a dining room through an archway to the left; to the right was a small sitting room with a larger living room beyond. After I'd hung up my hat and coat, Orlovska went into the sitting room. There was a long sofa facing a huge open fireplace with a freshly kindled blaze.

Orlovska spoke directly to me for the first time. She spoke excellent English.

"Make yourself at home. I'll be down in a few minutes. You'll find whisky and ice on the end table. I think there are some American cigarettes there, too."

She left the room then, and I heard her climb the stairs.

I needed a whisky badly at that point but the first thing I did was to reach for my gun and knock off the safety catch before I replaced it in the shoulder holster.

Then I tiptoed to the hallway. There wasn't a sound from upstairs. I went to the front door and turned the knob. It wasn't locked.

I walked softly over to the clothes rack, put on my hat and coat. I went to the front door, opened it, and stopped out on the porch. There wasn't a sound.

I started to pull the door shut behind me.

Where would I go once the door was closed? I was a good ten miles from the center of Budapest. I couldn't risk thumbing a ride even assuming there was any traffic at that time of the morning. Even if some motorists hadn't heard the broadcasts or seen the yellow posters, I couldn't attempt to pass the road-block. I'd have to walk but I couldn't go cross-country because of the snow and the highway was out.

And where would I go? Hiram Carr's? But he had said, "Whether you like it or not, you're going to see this thing through with us." He'd said, "You'd better make up your mind right now that there's nothing you can do to save Mademoiselle Torres without our help." Hiram Carr had sent me to the Arizona to meet Anna Orlovska. I'd met her and I had a chance to get the in-formation Carr wanted. Maybe I'd have to use threats. There was a loaded gun inside my jacket.

Without the help of Hiram Carr, there wasn't much I could do about finding Maria. And I knew that getting her out of the hands of Herr Doktor Wolfgang Schmidt had become more important to me than my original mission to Hungary to trace my brother Bob.

I went back inside and closed the door. I had just hung up my hat and coat again when I heard a door slam upstairs. I was pouring a drink when Orlovska en-tered the sitting room. She'd changed the white satin evening gown for a black lace negligee and she was something to look at.

I handed her my drink and mixed another.

"I must apologize again, Madame, for having been so inexcusably clumsy on the dance floor." The speech sounded like something out of a Victorian novel. I spoke English. There wasn't any reason why a Swiss shouldn't speak English.

Orlovska curled up on one end of the sofa. I sat

facing her at the other. I waited for her to start the conversation.

She said, "I always thought I was too tough to faint."

"We must have caught you off balance," I said. "Did you hit your head?"

Orlovska laughed.

"Off balance is right. And maybe I should have my head examined."

"I beg your pardon?"

"Stop it," she said. "The Russians tap my telephone and they open my mail but they haven't wired this place, not yet. We can talk frankly."

I waited for her to go on. She lit a cigarette.

"You must have known how closely they watch me," Orlovska said, "or you wouldn't have dreamed up that bumping act." She stared at the fire. "So," she said slowly, "you're really back from the grave?"

I'd thought perhaps I was crazy when I'd hopped in her car. Now I knew it.

"The grave?"

The flickering light from the fire made her face look hard. Now that I was close to her I could see she wasn't as young as I'd thought. Or else she'd lived in a hurry.

"I told you we can talk. There's nobody listening."

"I'm sorry," I said, "but I haven't the slightest notion of what you're talking about." What did she mean "back from the grave"? Did she know about the session at Dr. Schmidt's warehouse? Or the encounter in the Keleti station yards?

"I know why you've come to Budapest," she said, "al-

though I can't imagine how you got into the country."
Then she didn't know about Marcel Blaye's passport?
"But I don't blame you for coming. I'd do the same
thing in your place."

I poured myself another drink.

"Are you going to kill me?" Orlovska said.

"No," I said. "I assure you I haven't the slightest intention of killing you."

"Then what do you want?"

I wanted to know who had Marcel Blaye's Manila
envelope and where, but it wasn't the moment. First
I'd have to discover where and when I'd met Orlovska.

"Listen," she said when I didn't answer, "I won't try
to kid you. The Russians don't know anything about my
past. Lavrentiev thinks I spent the war in Poland."

Then we'd met during the war. But where? Orlovska
wasn't the kind I'd have forgotten. I tried to picture her
with black hair or red hair but it wasn't any good.

"I don't want Lavrentiev to know what happened,"
she said. She moved closer and put her hand on my
arm. "Please," she said. "I ditched Lavrentiev so I could
follow you when you left the Arizona. When I told
Lavrentiev to put you out, I hadn't seen your face. Oh,
he's drunk enough so he won't remember in the morning. But the gendarmes know I went after you because
I asked them to shout to attract your attention. The cop
who stopped you knows we're together. So does my
chauffeur. I've taken a great risk to bring you out here.
I didn't do it to play games."

"Why did you do it?" I said.

"I want to know your price."

"My price?"

"Don't be a fool." She stamped her foot. "The price of your silence."

What was I supposed to know about her that she was willing to pay to suppress? Why was she so afraid of what I might tell Lavrentiev?

"How did you know I was in Budapest?" she said. She poured herself another whisky and drank it straight. Maybe if she drank enough whisky I'd get the truth.

"Look," she said. "I don't expect you to forgive me. But it was all part of the war, wasn't it? Everybody was twisted, weren't they? Weren't they?"

"Yes," I said. "The whole world was pretty well upside down."

"Have you ever tried to understand the position of a woman like me? It wasn't easy to leave Warsaw and the life I'd always had. Oh, I know I can't expect you to believe anything good of me. But they promised me I could go back home, they said I could have my property back if I'd tell them where you were."

I handed her another drink.

"You can understand that, can't you? Can't you?"

"I don't understand at all," I said.

"You've got to understand. They'd have killed me if I hadn't told them where you were. You weren't in Budapest. You don't know. They went crazy when the steel works was bombed out."

"The what?" I said. "What are you talking about?"

"I said the Germans went mad when the Americans destroyed the Csepel Island factories. You couldn't talk to them. They knew you'd been shot down. They knew you were heading for Yugoslavia. I tell you it was my life or yours."

I grabbed her by the wrist.

"Who do you think I am?" I said. "Tell me. Who do you think I am?"

She screamed, "Stop it, you're hurting me."

"Answer me," I said. "What's my name?"

"Your name is Stodder," she said. "Your name is Bob Stodder."

I let go her wrist. She buried her face in her hands.

I turned my back on her and walked to the fireplace.

The next thing I knew, a voice from the doorway said, "Stay where you are, both of you. Put your hands over your heads and don't turn around."

I didn't have to turn around to recognize the voice of Herr Doktor Schmidt.

Chapter Twelve
TALK—OR DIE

Orlovska screamed again. She seemed to have limitless emotion.

"Yell your head off, Gnaedige Fräulein," Schmidt said sarcastically. "And don't waste your time pushing that button. Your servants are in no position to answer."

I wondered how long he'd been in the house and how much he'd heard of our conversation.

"Most interesting to find you two together," the doctor said. "It should prove most profitable—to me."

His voice came nearer. He had moved to the back of the sofa.

"Hermann will place two chairs against the far wall," he said. There followed the business of Hermann moving the chairs.

"You will kindly walk to the chairs. Don't drop your hands or I shall shoot. Perhaps, since Countess Orlovska is the hostess, you, Herr Stodder, should sit on her right. Yes, I think that appeals to my sense of humor."

Schmidt perched on the end of the sofa, his stumpy legs scarcely reaching the floor. The light from the fireplace cast dancing shadows on his gold-rimmed spectacles. He didn't bother to remove his gray Homburg.

This time, Schmidt and Hermann had come loaded for bear. The doctor carried an automatic pistol. Hermann carried a submachine gun.

"What have you done with Maria Torres?" I said. "Where is she?"

Schmidt grinned. "Aren't you being a little indelicate, Herr Stodder, bringing up the name of Mademoiselle Torres in front of the Countess Orlovska? I suppose, though, you Americans always manage to combine business with pleasure."

"Mademoiselle Torres?" Orlovska said. It hadn't taken her long to regain her composure. She was an old campaigner. "You mean Marcel Blaye's secretary?"

"The doctor is holding her prisoner," I said.

"Frankly," Orlovska said, "I don't care what happens to Mademoiselle Torres." She leaned forward in her chair. "But where is Marcel Blaye?"

Hermann snorted. Schmidt said, "Never mind, Hermann. It pleases me to let them talk. We've got lots of time." From the expression on the redheaded Hermann's ugly face, he couldn't wait to finish me off with his tommy gun.

"Doctor Schmidt murdered Marcel Blaye in Vienna," I said. "Ask him if you don't believe me."

Orlovska showed no emotion. She was plenty tough.

"That is something you might have difficulty in proving," the doctor said. "But as long as we're on the subject of Herr Blaye, you might explain to the countess how you came to enter Hungary on Blaye's passport. You might tell her how you came to know Mademoiselle Torres so well." He pushed his hat back on his bullet head. "And how you came into possession of the famous Manila envelope. That is a question that we shall have to discuss sooner or later."

"But I don't understand," Orlovska said. Astonishment was written all over her face. "What did you have to do with Marcel Blaye?"

"Nothing," I said. "I never heard of the man until the day before yesterday."

Schmidt was enjoying the situation thoroughly. He could hardly contain his laughter.

"He says he came to Hungary to trace his brother," the doctor said to Orlovska. "He says his brother was shot down in an American bombing plane during the war."

"Oh, my God," Orlovska said. "Then you aren't Bob Stodder?"

"My name is John Stodder," I said, "and I did come to try to find Bob. Thanks to you I know what happened. You sent him to his death."

The countess let loose with a string of unprintable words. "You tricked me," she said.

"I didn't trick you at all," I said. "I assure you it was a family resemblance and your own dirty conscience that made you talk."

Schmidt laughed. "I haven't enjoyed myself so much in years."

"So one of you killed Blaye?" Orlovska said. "How do you think you'll get away with it?"

"Doctor Schmidt also killed Major Strakhov," I said.

"But it's you the Russians are looking for," Schmidt said. "They seem to think you did it. I think you'd have some difficulty in proving otherwise. I assume you've seen the posters and heard the broadcasts?"

"Colonel Lavrentiev will have you both shot," Orlovska said. "He never asks for proof."

"I don't think your Colonel Lavrentiev will have anything to do with our little drama," Schmidt said. "I think we shall have solved our problems long before he sobers up."

"You don't think you can get away from this house?" the countess said. "My servants are armed."

"Your servants *were* armed," Schmidt said. "Hermann and I took the precaution of tying them securely before we joined your little party."

"My chauffeur is due back any minute."

Schmidt shook his head. "Ah, no, Gnaedige Fräulein. Your chauffeur has gone for the night. You see, he has been working for me for a long time. That's how you came to get such a capable man."

The doctor removed his spectacles and polished them with his handkerchief. He dropped the gun into his pocket. "I think Hermann has sufficient artillery for any situation," he said.

"Isn't that the telephone ringing?" Orlovska said.

"If it is," Dr. Schmidt said, "it's a miracle because Hermann cut the wires."

He pulled at his ear.

"I think we've had enough of this comedy," Schmidt said thoughtfully. "I think the time has come to get down to business.

"Herr Stodder, you were, shall we say, a guest of mine earlier this evening. I was foolish enough not to listen to Otto. I should have indulged his fancy. I think now he would have found a way to make you tell the truth. But I made one of the few mistakes of my life. I let you talk me into sending you into the railway yards with Hermann and Otto. I must admit I underestimated you. You led my men into an ambush, and it cost Otto his life."

"You told them to kill me when they got the envelope," I said. "I didn't find the envelope. It wasn't there. And you never had any intention of waiting at the coffeehouse with Maria Torres. You didn't wait five minutes after I left."

"I don't think we're interested in details," Schmidt said. "I don't know who your friends were but it isn't of the slightest importance at the moment."

He turned to Orlovska.

"This is the first time we've met," the doctor said, "although one could hardly say we were strangers. We've known about each other for a long time, haven't we?"

Orlovska didn't answer him. She didn't appear worried. I'm sure she expected help to arrive any minute although I can't imagine what she thought Hermann would do with that tommy gun if the Russians did come.

"You have put me to a great deal of trouble," Schmidt continued. "If it hadn't been for you, Marcel Blaye would be alive tonight."

Orlovska laughed. She was a cool cucumber, I'll say that for her. She said, "If you think you can pin a murder on me, you're crazy. Lavrentiev knows I haven't been out of Hungary in a year."

"You mustn't take me literally," Schmidt said patiently. "I killed Marcel Blaye. I killed him because he was a traitor and he deserved to die. But he sold out to the Russians because of you. You are a beautiful woman, Gnaedige Fräulein, and you know how to use your wits."

"Thank you," Orlovska said.

"Not at all," the doctor said. "But you've also got the morals of a pig."

The countess started to say something, but Schmidt stopped her with a wave of his hand.

"I know all about you so you can save your breath. You worked for the German Army during the war, here in Hungary. Then you went over to the Russians when the Red Army took over this country. I shouldn't be at all surprised if you had made a deal with Herr Stodder to work for the Americans.

"But all that is beside the point. You made a traitor out of Marcel Blaye. You arranged for him to sell out to the Russians."

Schmidt resumed his perch on the end of the sofa.

"When Marcel Blaye left Geneva, he carried a Manila envelope. He was planning to deliver it to Colonel Lavrentiev through the Countess Orlovska.

"Unfortunately, the envelope was not among Blaye's possessions when he and I came face to face in Vienna. Maria Torres carried it onto the Orient Express. It was on her person when she and Herr Stodder resumed their journey from the frontier with Major Strakhov."

He took his gun from his pocket. "Hermann," he said, "you will get two lengths of rope from the car. And my black bag." He turned back to Orlovska and me. "I call it my doctor bag. You'd be surprised how useful it is in emergencies."

Schmidt knocked the safety catch off his gun.

"The point is," he said, "that I want that envelope. And I assure you I am quite prepared to go to any lengths to get it."

"I don't know what you're talking about," Orlovska said but she didn't say it with the assurance she'd had five minutes earlier.

"I told you I don't know where the envelope is," I said. I started to say that I had hoped to find out from Orlovska but I managed to check my tongue in time.

Hermann was back in a minute. While Schmidt covered us, Hermann roped first Orlovska, then me to our chairs, our hands tied behind our backs. The red-headed goon took over again with the submachine gun, and Schmidt emptied the contents of the black bag on the rug in front of us. There must have been a couple of dozen stainless-steel instruments, things that resembled dentist's pliers and surgeon's scalpels. Schmidt arranged them in a neat row with loving care.

"Unhappily for you two," he said, "I did not arrive early enough to hear your entire conversation. If I had, I should probably not have to threaten drastic measures to get the truth from you.

"But, as I've already informed you, I want that Manila envelope. I happen to want it immediately. It is immaterial to me from which of you I get the truth. If you care to discuss it among yourselves, I shall be quite content."

The doctor drew his watch from his pocket.

"I'll allow you three minutes to decide who'll tell me the truth," he said. "I don't think you'll need more time."

He motioned to Hermann, and they went into a huddle at the far end of the room. I couldn't hear what the doctor was saying but I was very conscious of the seconds ticking away.

The sight of Schmidt's instruments on the floor and the growing realization that help was a long way off had pretty well ended Orlovska's arrogance. Her fear of me when she thought I was my brother whom she had betrayed, her terror at the thought that I planned to reveal her Nazi associations to the Russians, had disappeared when she'd learned I was wanted for the death of Strakhov. She must have figured then that Lavrentiev wouldn't have believed anything I told him about her. But now that she was convinced that Schmidt meant business, she was fast approaching a collapse.

"What is he going to do?" she said. "What will happen to us?" She hardly spoke above a whisper.

I wasn't feeling too courageous myself at that moment but I was damned if I was going to let her know it.

"He's going to use those instruments unless you tell him where to find Blaye's envelope," I said. "I don't imagine we'll enjoy the performance."

Orlovska shuddered. "But I don't know anything about it. I thought Blaye had it. I thought Blaye had brought it into Hungary. I didn't know it was you. I thought Blaye had decided to welsh on the agreement. I was sure Maria Torres had talked him into welshing."

"Think fast," I said. "Try to remember what Lavrentiev told you."

I had to know what she knew. Not because I wanted her to tell Schmidt. The moment the doctor learned the truth would be the moment he'd turn Hermann loose with the tommy gun. The truth would be our death sentence. The only hope we had was to find the truth, then use it as a defensive weapon against Schmidt. As long as he thought we were holding out on him, he'd keep us alive. It was a weird situation where I had to concern myself with the life of the woman who had sent my brother to his death. But I knew my salvation depended on hers. For the moment.

"Quick," I said. "What happened today? What did Lavrentiev tell you? We haven't much time."

The shiny instruments on the floor seemed to fascinate her the way a serpent is supposed to hypnotize a rabbit. She'd gotten by, all her life, on her physical charm and her wits. For the first time, she was facing an opponent who wasn't interested.

"We expected Blaye on the afternoon train," she said slowly. "Lavrentiev and I went to Kcleti to meet Strakhov and Blaye and Mademoiselle Torres."

"What happened?" I said. "What did you do?" Schmidt was still talking to Hermann in low tones.

"Nothing," she said. "You didn't arrive." It was like the cub reporter who phoned the office to say there was no story because the bride hadn't shown up at the wedding.

"You must have done something," I said. "What did you do when you heard Strakhov had been murdered?"

"My God," Orlovska said. "What difference does it make?"

"Tell me," I said. "What did you and Lavrentiev do when you heard Strakhov was dead?"

"Lavrentiev ordered an alarm broadcast for you and Maria Torres."

"Then what did you do?" I said. "You've got to think faster."

"Then we went to Jozsefvaros." Jozsefvaros is a freight station between suburban Kelenfold, where Maria and I and Schmidt had left the train, and the main Keleti terminal.

"Jozsefvaros?" I said. "Why did you go there?"

"That's where the car was."

"What car?"

"The railroad car where Strakhov was murdered. They took it to Jozsefvaros. They took it away from Keleti as soon as the train was empty.

"What railroad car?" she said. "My God, how stupid can you get?"

Chapter Thirteen

HORRIBLE TORTURE

I could get pretty stupid. But so could Hiram Carr and Herr Doktor Schmidt. All three of us had possessed the answer to the whereabouts of the Manila envelope and none of us had recognized it.

Obviously the MVD would want to photograph Strakhov's body and its position. They'd try to get fingerprints. They'd examine the luggage we'd left behind, the clothing that had been scattered by Schmidt in his frantic search for the envelope after the murder. The natural course was to haul the death car to another station; there would be too many curious travelers in Keleti and it would hardly be convenient to lug cameras, lights, and fingerprint equipment into the snowbound yards.

I had counted three Austrian carriages in the yards. But there had been plenty of time to substitute another car in the train for the run back to Vienna. That accounted for the fact that the sticker *Reserved for the Embassy of the USSR* hadn't been in any of the cars I'd searched with Hermann and Otto. The sticker hadn't been removed but the carriage had.

Marcel Blaye's envelope with Dr. Schmidt's secrets

was still behind the cushion in a first-class Austrian railway car, in a compartment decorated with the scenic delights of Salzburg and Innsbruck. Because the MVD had no reason to look for the envelope in another compartment. The killer, still known officially as Marcel Blaye, the identification reinforced by the tags on my bags and the labels in my clothing, would have vanished with the envelope at Kelenfold. It was his property. What reason would he have to leave it behind? Why murder, why flight, except to welsh on his deal?

Hiram Carr knew about the envelope because he'd seen me duck into the end compartment. Schmidt knew I'd left it in the car because I'd told him. But we'd searched the wrong carriages in the Keleti yards. The right one was a mile away, sealed and guarded on a freight-station sidetrack by the Russians, who didn't know what they had.

I was sure Orlovska hadn't realized the significance of what she'd told me. Even if she'd possessed the background information to make two and two equal four, her nervous and mental state at the moment was hardly conducive to thought. The sight of the German doctor's stainless-steel instruments and the thought of what he intended to do with them threatened to reduce her to a gibbering idiot.

Schmidt and Hermann recrossed the room to us.

"So," the doctor said, "you have made up your minds to tell me everything." It wasn't a question. There just hadn't been any room in his mind for doubt.

I didn't answer. Apparently Orlovska was too frightened for speech. But Schmidt had time.

"You know," he said with a broad grin, "this is a most amusing situation. I am a German. Countess Orlovska works for the Russians, and Herr Stodder is an American. You represent Germany's conquerors in the recent, shall we say, battle. Yet you are both my prisoners, answerable to my commands. Shall we call it prophetic symbolism?"

The uneasy suspicion had been growing in my mind, ever since the doctor took Maria and me to his warehouse hideout, that he was more than just a die-hard German nationalist. I had begun to believe he was a madman.

Schmidt wiped his spectacles again. His tiny pig eyes gleamed.

"Now," he said. "You will please tell me what you have done with Marcel Blaye's envelope."

"I know where it is," I said.

"Where?"

"It's in the railway car where I left it," I said.

Schmidt hit me across the face with the back of his hand.

"You told me that a few hours ago," the doctor said. "How stupid do you think I am? You led one of my men to his death because I took a chance on that story. Oh, no, Herr Stodder, you will have to do better than that. Where is the envelope?"

"I just told you," I said.

I still don't think it was a bad idea. He'd been burned once. He wouldn't believe it again unless—unless Orlovska explained it to him. He'd use those instruments on us but he'd be very careful to keep us alive as long as he thought we were holding back on him. Looking back, I think it was smart to tell him right away. He wouldn't credit any confession I would make under torture. And I didn't know what to do at that moment if it wasn't to stall for time.

Schmidt turned to Orlovska. She was wide-eyed with fear.

"Speak up, Gnaedige Fräulein," the doctor said. "Where is the Manila envelope?"

"I don't know," Orlovska said. "I don't know. I don't know."

The doctor stepped back and looked at us both.

"So," he said. "Very well. We shall proceed with our little entertainment. I think it only fair to tell you that I am an expert. You see, as a graduate veterinarian I served some years at Dachau."

The doctor and Hermann picked me up in my chair and carried me into the center of the room. I was to get the first workout. Schmidt must have figured that if I didn't know where the envelope was, the sight of my suffering would cause Orlovska to break down before her turn arrived.

The first time I'd been the doctor's prisoner I'd told him truthfully that I wasn't the least interested in Marcel Blaye's envelope. I'd blurted out the real story of my visit to Hungary. I'd told him everything and I'd offered to get the envelope and turn it over to him. All I'd asked in return was the release of Maria Torres and myself so that Maria could return safely to Geneva while I started my search for my brother.

Now I knew what had happened to Bob. The female

Judas who had sold him for German promises was only a few feet away from me, bound like me and about to be tortured by a madman. I didn't care what happened to her but I did care about what Schmidt should learn. There was loyalty to Hiram Carr and to my country. Carr had saved my life. And there was loyalty to Maria Torres and a good deal more than loyalty, too. Schmidt had double-crossed us both. He never had any intention of freeing us in return for the cursed envelope. He'd told Hermann and Otto to shoot me to death in the railway yards as soon as I handed over the envelope. He'd kidnapped Maria, maybe even given her the treatment he was about to administer to me.

Schmidt selected a gleaming instrument from the row on the floor. He held it in front of the light so that Orlovska and I might have a good look. It was a long, thin steel needle.

"This is something I worked out myself," the doctor said. "I think you'll appreciate my ingenuity."

Time from then on was only a blur. Each time I fainted, Hermann threw cold water in my face to revive me. There was nothing brave about me. I repeated the truth and Schmidt didn't believe it. He used half a dozen instruments. There came a time when I prayed that he'd recognize the truth and let me remain unconscious. But I couldn't tell him about the Austrian coach that had been hauled to Jozsefvaros. The words came readily to my lips. It was only that each time I gathered strength to utter them I saw the face of Maria Torres, the trusting wide-set black eyes, the slightly hollowed cheeks, and the firm line of her jaw, the way she'd believed me when I'd told my story, the way she'd drawn my face down to hers to kiss me.

I was scarcely aware of being moved back to the wall; I suppose I guessed vaguely that I was being given a breathing-spell when Orlovska's screams told me she was next. I was drugged with pain. It was some minutes before I managed to raise my head.

I don't know whether I've explained that the sitting room, like the hallway, ran the full depth of the house. I think that was true of all the rooms on the ground floor. There were the usual windows in the front of the house. There were French doors in the back, opening onto a porch which ran the width of the building.

When Schmidt and Hermann had carried me back from the center of the room, they had placed my chair in front of one of the French windows.

It was almost worse to hear Orlovska's agony than it had been to be on the receiving end of the doctor's entertainment. I kept telling myself she was only getting for the first time what she had helped hand out a dozen times. She had sent my brother to his death. She was a woman completely without principle, a mercenary who used her body and her wits in the service of the highest bidder. Still she was a woman.

"You lousy bastard," I called to Schmidt. It wasn't the first name I'd used for him. "She doesn't know anything. There isn't a thing she can tell you. I've told you the truth. For God's sake, let her alone."

Schmidt didn't bother to answer. But Hermann jammed the butt of his tommy gun into my stomach, and I passed out again. When I came to, he said, "That's for Otto."

The doctor let up on Orlovska every minute or so.

"Where is the envelope? What did you do with the envelope? Where is it?"

Orlovska shook her head.

"Did you find it in the railway car?" When she didn't answer, he slapped her face.

"Did Colonel Lavrentiev find it in the railway car?" She shook her head.

"Is it here? Did Stodder bring it here?"

"Oh, my God," Orlovska said. I could hardly hear her voice.

"Was it on Strakhov's body? Have the Russians got it?"

Schmidt slapped her again. Orlovska said, "No."

"What did Stodder tell you about the envelope? What did he say? What did he tell you about it?"

But Orlovska was unconscious.

It was at that moment that I became aware of sound behind me, on the other side of the French window. Someone or something was walking on the wooden porch.

Chapter Fourteen
DRUGGED WITH PAIN

I thought my imagination was playing tricks on me. I'd taken terrific punishment.

I heard the sound again. It could have been a shutter creaking in the wind.

Hermann brought Orlovska around with the water treatment.

"Where is the envelope?" Schmidt said again. Why didn't the bastard put it to music? "What did you do with the envelope?"

I was sure I heard the sound once more on the porch behind me. It was probably a dog seeking shelter from the snow.

"Did you visit the railroad car?"

I thought, *Here it comes.*

Orlovska said yes.

"Did you go with Colonel Lavrentiev?"

I held my breath.

Orlovska nodded her head.

I felt that someone was looking through the window in back of me. I thought my fevered imagination was running wild.

"When did you go with Lavrentiev?" Schmidt asked Orlovska.

"This evening," she said in a barely audible voice. "Early in the evening."

The doctor's next question had to be "Where?" I listened but there was no sound from the porch behind me save the rustling of the wind.

"While the train was in the station?" the doctor said. "Answer me. While the train was in the Keleti station?" I figured he was trying to establish the time of her visit.

"No," Orlovska said.

"Then you boarded the train in the yards?" He wanted to know whether she and the chief of the MVD had visited the train before or after I had gone with his two goons.

The countess shook her head.

"I see we shall have to employ more drastic treatment," Schmidt said, "until you decide which it is. You tell me you boarded the train with Lavrentiev. You refuse to tell where or when."

He picked up another instrument from the rug. It looked like an enormous pair of pliers, a machine to break bones. He held it in front of Orlovska and slapped her ashen face until she raised her head and opened her eyes.

"Jozsefvaros," she said.

Schmidt slapped her again. "Fool. Passenger trains don't stop at Jozsefvaros."

Hermann, who'd been standing in the doorway at the other end of the room from me, interrupted.

"Excellenz, one moment."

"What is it, Hermann?"

"Excellenz, I hear noise. There is someone outside, Excellenz.."

Hermann was right. There was someone outside. He picked that moment to send a bullet through one of the front windows, shattering the glass. The bullet buried itself in the ceiling.

The sound of voices speaking Russian came through the broken window.

Schmidt switched out the lights.

There was a second shot through the window. Hermann fired a burst from his tommy gun.

The voices grew louder, but I couldn't make out what they were saying. I didn't make much effort. Rescue by the Russians could only mean more trouble for me. It was fine for Orlovska who was sobbing hysterically. But, as far as I was concerned, there wasn't much difference between Lavrentiev and Schmidt. At least I had felt sure that Schmidt would keep me alive until he found the Manila envelope. There would be no reason for the MVD to spare my life; Orlovska could tell them quickly where to find Blaye's papers. If I lived even that long. I told you the doctor and Hermann had placed me in front of the window, which was in a direct line with the shattered front window. Sooner or later the Russians would probably send a bullet straight through that window.

Instead of burying itself in the ceiling, it would bury itself in me. Schmidt and Hermann, in any event, couldn't hope to hold out for any length of time. The best they could do would be to take a few Russians with them. The latter couldn't lose even if it meant destroying the building.

Schmidt shouted, "Hermann."

"Hier, Excellenz."

"They will try to come through this window. Move into the hallway. Shoot when they come through the window."

"Ja wohl, Excellenz."

Schmidt moved into the opposite corner. I saw his shadow cross the second window. I could still hear the Russian voices. I figured they were deciding a plan of attack.

The next bullet came through the window nearest the doctor. He didn't fire in return. He'd apparently decided to wait until they stormed the place. He must have guessed the house was surrounded. I don't think he had heard the sounds that I had heard from the back porch but he knew from the sounds of the voices outside that the Russians were there in strength.

The voices in front of the building became louder.

"Now," Schmidt shouted to Hermann. "They will come now."

There was another bullet through the window nearest Hermann. The redheaded German said, "That one was close, Excellenz."

Either his trigger finger slipped or he thought he saw the Russians approaching the window because he fired another burst from the tommy gun.

The next thing I knew, someone clapped a huge hand over my mouth. I tried to yell, but the sound was drowned by the explosions from Hermann's gun. My ropes were so tight I couldn't struggle.

I felt myself lifted into the air, chair and all. My head whirled. I went through the French window which had opened behind me. I heard Orlovska scream.

I couldn't see who was carrying me, someone of enormous strength.

I was carried the length of the porch and into the deep snow at the end.

There was a stand of pines a short way from the end of the house. We had almost reached the shelter of the trees when the shots came from the house.

I felt myself plunging into space. I landed with a sickening thud in the snow. I'd either been dropped so whoever was carrying me could fire back at the house or else he'd been hit.

There were answering shots but they came from somewhere off to the right.

The next thing I knew, my ropes had been cut and I rolled free of the heavy chair. Then someone picked me up with the fireman's hold, and we moved again toward the shelter of the pines but slower and less steadily than before.

When we were well inside the woods, the man who had been carrying me set me on my feet. My legs gave way under me but he managed to prop me against a tree. It was darker than the inside of my pocket.

I expected to be left there. I thought he might be going back to the house for Orlovska or to get first aid for his wound; I was sure he'd been hit when he let me drop in the snow. But he stuck a cigarette in my mouth. I heard him mutter something and I figured he couldn't find a match.

"I've got a match," I said in Russian. It's one of the first phrases in the book. "In my left pocket." I couldn't have held even a matchbox. Schmidt had ripped my hands.

I felt a hand in my pocket. Then I heard a match strike. It burst into flame. It lit my cigarette. I took a couple of deep puffs.

The hand drew back the lighted match. I saw the face of my rescuer, and the cigarette dropped from my lips into the snow.

I had expected to see a Russian soldier or a Hungarian gendarme. But the man standing next to me was neither. He was a tall, rawboned man with a wide smile.

It was Hiram Carr's butler, Walter.

Chapter Fifteen
SEARCH FOR A GIRL

"Please be quiet, Mr. Stodder," Walter said softly. "They may try to follow our tracks in the snow." He put another cigarette in my mouth and lit it.

"But you're hurt," I said. "They must have hit you. You've got to have help."

"I'm all right," Walter said. "We'll move in a few minutes. Those krauts must have given you a bad time, Mr. Stodder." My boiled shirt was spattered with blood.

There were a dozen questions I wanted to ask. Where was Hiram Carr? How had Walter known the Russians would attack the house? How had he and Carr known where I was?

We stood in silence under the tree in the darkness for ten minutes or so. There was no sound from the direction of the house. Maybe Schmidt and Hermann had surrendered, but I thought it unlikely. Either the Russians had killed both the Germans or they had ceased fire to plan a new attack.

There was a road somewhere close behind us. We heard a car approach. I thought it was going to stop, that perhaps the Russians were bringing up more men.

They could be looking for me. But the car passed without slowing, and then we heard its horn off in the distance.

"We'll go now," Walter said. "It isn't far."

He started to pick me up, but I told him I could walk. He hadn't noticed my feet were bare and still bleeding. We had only about fifty feet to go to the road but it took us a long time to find our way around the trees in the inky darkness. I fell half a dozen times.

"You wait here, Mr. Stodder," Walter said. "Everything's all right. I'll be back for you directly." The first streaks of dawn were lightening the sky.

Someone whistled down the road, in the direction Walter had taken, the first few bars of "Dixie," and in a few minutes a car appeared out of the morning mist.

When the car came abreast of where I was sitting, Walter hopped off the running board to help me in. Hiram, still in his pea jacket and coonskin cap, was behind the wheel. Teensy was beside him, still in her ski costume, the two bright spots of orange rouge gray in the morning light.

Teensy winced when she saw my hands and feet, but neither she nor her husband commented. There wasn't any small talk. Hiram got right to the point.

"Where is the envelope? Did you find out from Orlovska?"

I noticed we were driving farther away from Budapest, toward the west. The wild idea entered my head that we were heading for Vienna, that this was the first step in leaving Hungary.

"Where are you going?" I said. "We've got to get back to Budapest. You promised me you'd help me find Maria. I've done what you asked. You can't let me down."

Hiram said quietly, "Nobody's letting you down. We wouldn't have been here if we were going to let you down. But the roadblock is still in back of us. We'd never get through it now. We'll have to take another road back to Budapest. First we've got to get you and Walter to a doctor."

"All right," I said. "Yes, I know where the envelope is. It's where I left it."

I saw Hiram glance at Teensy as if he thought my mind was wandering as a result of Schmidt's treatment. Walter must have told him what he'd seen through the window.

"That's where it is," I said. "Don't worry, I'm not crazy. The Russians moved the car. They took it off the train and moved it to Jozsefvaros. They took it away after you two left the train at Keleti. We looked in the wrong cars, that's all."

"Did Orlovska tell you that?" Hiram asked.

"Yes," I said.

"Then the envelope isn't there any more. If she knew it, Lavrentiev did, too."

"No," I said. "She knew the car was moved because she and Lavrentiev went through it at Jozsefvaros. But they didn't know about the envelope. She told Schmidt about the car being moved, though, and he knew the envelope was there."

I filled them in on what had happened after Walter left me near the Arizona.

"How did you know the Russians were going to attack the house?" I said.

"We didn't," Teensy said. Hiram laughed.

"How did you get there at the same time?"

"A little invention of this corny husband of mine," Teensy said. She pinched his cheek, and he gurgled like a happy child.

"What invention?" I said. "What did an invention have to do with it?" I was beaten up and worn out and hardly in the mood for conundrums. "Walter got me out the back window because Schmidt and Hermann were busy with the Russians in front."

Hiram giggled. I could have murdered him with pleasure at that point.

"That's correct," Teensy said, "only there weren't any Russians."

"I'm not crazy," I said. "I heard them in front of the house."

"Phonograph record," Teensy said.

"What?"

"It worked, didn't it?" Hiram said gleefully. "It fooled you and the Germans, didn't it?"

"Phonograph record," Teensy said. "Schmidt will be quite annoyed when he finds it.

"You see, Mr. Stodder, I told you Hiram is an incurable gadgeteer. He figured this out a long time ago. These new long playing machines in small sizes are just what he needed."

"Tell him about the voices he heard," Hiram said.

"Oh, those were Russians cheering Stalin at a May Day parade," Teensy said. "Hiram recorded them from a Moscow radio program."

"I've seen everything," I said. "But what about the shots that came in the front windows?"

"That was me," Teensy said, "while Walter worked around to the back porch. I might say it took some shooting, too, so I wouldn't hit you. Had to lie flat on my stomach in the snow so the bullets would hit the ceiling."

"So there weren't any Russians there at all?" I said. "That means Schmidt will get away."

"Maybe," Hiram said, "but he'll have a hell of a time. We put his car where he won't find it in a hurry and we shot all four tires to shreds. I think perhaps the Russians will get him before he finds the car."

"I thought you said they weren't around?"

"They weren't," Teensy said, "but they will be soon. You see, Hiram called them while Walter was bringing you out to the road."

"What do we do about Maria?" I said.

"We can't do anything until tonight," Hiram said. "We'll have to lay low today. Even if we dared, I don't think any doctor will let you move without a long sleep."

I don't know how long we drove. I managed to doze off despite my nerves. When I woke, the sun was in the sky. The car had stopped in the cobblestoned courtyard of what I took to be a country inn. A smiling Hungarian couple, whom I immediately supposed to be the proprietor and his wife, such being the inevitable pattern of life in a country inn, greeted Hiram and Teensy and showed me to a room.

I was put to bed, and they brought me breakfast, but I had little appetite. Hiram produced a doctor who dressed my wounds and filled me with sedatives. He said Walter had been shot in the leg but luckily it was only a flesh wound.

I slept the day through and awoke without that sense of depression which had taken hold when Maria disappeared. The prospect of doing something about finding her made me eager to start, although I couldn't do much walking or hold a gun in my hands. Speaking of guns, I remarked for the first time that Schmidt hadn't searched me at Orlovska's, and the gun Carr gave me had remained inside my jacket all the time.

Someone had removed my dinner jacket and substituted the clothes I had left at Carr's. The contents of my pockets had been emptied on the bureau. I remembered Ilonka dropping something in my pocket just as I was booted out of the Arizona by Lavrentiev's orderly. It stared back at me in the dim light of the room— Ilonka's blue glass eye, the good eye that fights the evil eye. It amused me, but I slipped it in my pocket when I had finished dressing.

I made my way down the stairs, a step at a time, to find Walter in the huge living room, seated in front of the open fire. Hiram and Teensy joined us in a few minutes. After a quick dinner, we shook hands with the proprietor and his wife and drove off in Hiram's car.

"What's the setup?" I said. "They've got a lot of guts

to take us in. What happens if the Russians catch them?"

Hiram took one hand off the wheel and drew it across his neck.

"But there are thousands like them in the countries behind the Iron Curtain," Hiram said, "decent people who figure they haven't anything to lose. These Communist regimes, these so-called People's Democracies, are run by the gutter element in all these Eastern European countries. People like the couple you just saw fought the Germans when they overran these countries. They don't see much difference between being managed from Berlin or Moscow."

"But I don't see why they should take their lives in their hands," I said. "Suppose a Russian patrol had walked into the place while we were there?"

"They'd have had a tough time finding us," Hiram said. "Those old buildings have a dozen hiding places. The proprietor's neighbors would have warned him the moment Russian or Hungarian police approached within a mile of the place."

"When'd they set that up?" I asked.

"It's been going on for hundreds of years. People in these countries have been hiding from one invader or another since the beginning of history. Take the Hungarians. They've been occupied by Romans, Huns, Slavs, Tartars, Turks, Rumanians, Austrians, and half a dozen others. They've fought them all and they've seen them all depart. Why should they accept the Russians any more than the others?"

"Where are we going?" I said.

"Matyasfold," Hiram said. "We'll start there, anyway."

When Schmidt had taken Maria and me to the tenement on Mexikoi ut he'd told Hermann to drive the Russian staff car "to Felix in Matyasfold." Felix would give the redheaded German civilian clothes and phony papers for himself and Otto as well as a car. I'd mentioned the fact to Hiram when I'd first gone to his home, and he had put two of his men on the job of watching Matyasfold, a town some ten miles from the Budapest city limits.

I was surprised that Hiram had put searching for Maria ahead of any attempt to get Marcel Blaye's Manila envelope from the railway car at Jozsefvaros. Not that he hadn't made me a promise. I guessed he figured the Russians had grabbed Schmidt when they'd arrived at Orlovska's and there was no hurry about the envelope. I'd told Hiram I was sure the countess, providing Schmidt hadn't killed her after my escape, couldn't reveal the secret because she hadn't realized what she had told me.

Carr must have read my mind because he said, "If you're right about that damned envelope, we've got a lousy job ahead of us. They'll have a dozen armed men around that car. They'll keep it there and they won't move it until they've hanged somebody for murdering Strakhov."

Teensy put it frankly. "If Hiram wasn't stumped we wouldn't be going to Matyasfold instead. But he'll think of something. He always has."

I wondered how much longer Hiram Carr could keep himself out of 60 Stalin ut, diplomatic passport or not.

The MVD certainly knew why he was in Budapest. They watch all foreigners, and diplomats twice as much. They'd long since learned Hiram wasn't an agricultural expert, that his legation job was a blind. Colonel Lavrentiev might get plastered nights at the Arizona but he was plenty smart, and so was his staff. It didn't occur to me at the moment that the Russians might be biding their time, waiting until they could grab all of us in one haul.

There wasn't any doubt of Carr's purpose in heading for Matyasfold. The rescue of a Spanish girl named Maria Torres had no meaning for him. She was strictly incidental. He wanted all the information he could gather on Schmidt and his gang, everything he could dig up on the underground German scientists. He thought he could learn from whoever was holding her prisoner for Schmidt. It didn't occur to either of us at that moment that Maria might not be alive.

We took long enough to return to Budapest, hitting the Danube far to the south of the city, then doubling back along the river. Hiram didn't dare try to pass the roadblocks in the Buda hills. When we had crossed the Danube, Hiram made a wide detour around the city to reach Matyasfold to the east. We never once saw a policeman, except for those on traffic duty. It was almost as if they'd been moved out of our path by design and it was unnatural enough to give me a sense of foreboding. We'd had too easy a time since Walter carried me from Orlovska's house. It was too good to last.

Matyasfold is one of those undistinguished towns, half city, half country, that you find near big cities all over the world. On the high-speed trolley line from Budapest, it's an ideal community for white-collar workers who can't afford city rents. At the beginning of the war, the Hungarians built an airport for the defense of Budapest. Then German fighter squadrons moved in. After the war, the Russian air force took over.

When we were a couple of miles from Matyasfold, Hiram changed places with Teensy. While she drove, he talked.

"After you told me how Schmidt had instructed Hermann to go to Matyasfold," Hiram said to me, "I put two of my men on the job.

"Felix isn't too common a name in Hungary. But my men could have spent a month finding the right Felix if that was all I gave them to go on. Do you remember what Schmidt told Hermann?"

"Of course," I said. "I remember the conversation almost exactly. After all, it was only yesterday." I could hardly believe that only twenty-four hours had passed since Maria and I had left the train at Kelenfold only to fall into the hands of the Nazi doctor. "Schmidt said, 'I want that car moved from here immediately. It is much too dangerous. You will drive it to Felix in Matyasfold.' "

"Do you remember what else Schmidt told Hermann?"

"He said, 'You will give your uniform to Felix. He will return your civilian clothes and the necessary documents. He will also give you clothes and documents for Otto.' Then he said, 'If you are stopped by police, you will tell them you are Frau Hoffmeyer's nephew.' "

Hiram said, "What does that conversation tell you about Felix?"

"Well," I said. "It means that Felix is one of Schmidt's agents."

"That's hardly a discovery," Hiram said. I didn't see why it amused him.

"It meant that Felix, whoever he is, was in a position to supply civilian clothes to Hermann. It meant he had facilities for forging documents."

"Or stealing them," Hiram said. "But don't you see the most important clue to the identity of Felix?"

"What do you mean?" I said.

"The car," he said, "the Russian army car."

"Schmidt told Hermann to hand it over to Felix."

"That's correct," Hiram said. "If it were only a question of faked documents or civilian clothes, Felix could be almost anybody. A shopkeeper, for instance, the postman, or the tax collector. But it isn't normal for such persons to have army staff cars and it isn't easy to hide one. Garage people can't disguise an army car with a coat of paint the way they do stolen stock cars. Anybody can dispose of a uniform like Hermann's but not automobiles with army insignia.

"The more I thought about that angle, the more I figured Felix had to be someone whose possession of a Red Army car wouldn't excite suspicion and someone who had access to official documents at the same time. It seemed to me we were looking for a Red Army officer and a fairly high one at that.

"I think we'll find that Doctor Schmidt's agent, the Felix who is stooge for the Nazi Bruderschaft, is pretty close to the commander of the Russian air base right here in Matyasfold."

"How do you know Schmidt brought Maria out here?" I said.

"I don't," Hiram said, "but we've got to start looking somewhere, don't we?"

Chapter Sixteen
ON GUARD

I had visions of Hiram, Teensy, Walter, and me driving up to the main gate of the air base to attack the garrison. The six-foot Teensy with her bleached-blond hair, little Hiram in his coonskin cap, Walter, the perpetually smiling ex-prizefighter with a bum leg, and John Stodder alias Marcel Blaye alias Jean Stodder, the involuntary watch and clock salesman whose bandaged hands couldn't hold a gun. Coxey's Army would have looked like a West Point color guard alongside us. It was the strangest American expeditionary force on record.

"What are we going to do?" I asked Hiram.

"Call on a friend of mine for a cup of coffee."

Hiram told Teensy to turn off the main highway into the Kossuth Lajos utca, about half a mile short of the air base. The car skidded and spun wildly in the narrow, rutted road, but we had less than half a block to go. The street was lined on both sides with identical crackerbox bungalows, the Hungarian equivalent of a hundred communities along the Long Island Rail Road.

"It's all right," Hiram said. "Let's go in."

I couldn't figure how he knew until I noticed the

shade was half raised in one of the windows of the bungalow we were entering.

"You're a new member of the agricultural attaché's staff," Hiram said.

"I don't know the difference between timothy and trailing arbutus," I said.

"Never mind," said Hiram. "Neither do I. Your hands and feet were frostbitten when you went skiing. That's how Walter hurt his leg."

"That gives American skiers a fine reputation," I said. "Incidentally, what's my name?"

"John Stodder," he said. "I've got papers to prove it."

I couldn't understand why the briefing, if we were visiting one of Hiram's agents, until we went inside the house. We were introduced in turn to Bela Szabo, his wife and seven children, the wife's mother, somebody's brother-in-law, and the serving girl who insisted on kissing everybody's hand.

It seemed that Mrs. Szabo sewed for Teensy, and there were a couple of dresses ready to try on. The two women vanished into a back room, Hiram and Papa Szabo, a gaunt, bearded, melancholy man, repaired to the small porch to smoke a cigar, and Walter and I were left with the seven children, Mrs. Szabo's mother, and the unidentified brother-in-law who volunteered to play the accordion. The serving girl, who answered to the name of Lilli, passed the apricot brandy.

I tried to answer Mrs. Szabo's mother's questions about America, but my mind was on Maria. Now that there was a possibility I might see her again, perhaps within a few hours, my feelings were uncertain. I'd thought of little else since I left her outside the coffee-house with Schmidt. With reunion perhaps close at hand, I was filled with misgivings.

After all, what did I know about Maria Torres except what she herself had told me? How did I know she hadn't voluntarily left the coffeehouse with the German doctor without waiting for me? What proof did I have, aside from the background she had given me, for believing she was a prisoner of Schmidt and not an accomplice?

I remembered how surprised I'd been when she'd responded to Schmidt's command in German at Kelenfold to "Pick up your baggage," although she'd told me she understood no German. There was no sign of emotion in her lovely face at that moment, none of the terror she'd displayed when she'd first sighted Schmidt aboard the Orient Express. I remembered how calm she'd been in the warehouse on Mexikoi ut and how I'd mistrusted her show of nerves when we'd met on the Orient. I'd started to put her down as a girl with too much imagination and too little control of herself. Maybe I'd been right. Maybe it had been clever acting.

But that didn't make sense, either. She'd followed me off the Orient, with all the danger that involved. She'd played my game with Major Strakhov. She'd stuck by me when I decided to leave the train at Kelenfold. And hadn't she thrown her arms around my neck and kissed me when I left her to enter the Keleti yards? Hadn't she tried to go with me?

"I don't get it." I said it out loud in English because Mrs. Szabo's mother said in Hungarian, "I beg your pardon?"

"I'm sorry," I said. "I don't know what I was thinking of. You were asking me about the Brooklyn Bridge?" The unidentified brother-in-law promptly pumped out an off-key rendition of "The Sidewalks of New York," and Papa Szabo stuck his head in the door to tell him to be careful because the People's Democracy does not favor fraternization with foreigners. Then Walter, who didn't speak a word of Hungarian, told the fascinated children, who didn't understand a word of English, the story of Br'er Rabbit.

I stood by during endless handshaking and the patting of small heads, toasts in apricot brandy, and more hand kissing by the serving girl who got the customary quarter from each of us in tips. Then we left.

Hiram turned the car around after some difficulty, and we drove back to the main highway to head in the direction of the Russian air base.

"I thought you said we were going for a cup of coffee," I said.

"There isn't any coffee in the whole of Hungary," Hiram said. "Haven't you noticed?"

"How would I notice?" I said. "Except for a warehouse, a nightclub, several assorted homes, and a country inn, I might as well have gone through Budapest in a fast train. I'd like to see what the city's like these days."

"Not this trip," Hiram said. He started to add something but he shut up. He wasn't kidding me. I knew the chances were pretty slim I'd ever get out of the country alive, much less see the sights of Budapest. He and Teensy had diplomatic status. At the worst, they'd be jailed until Washington locked up a Russian diplomat and arranged an exchange. Walter and I came under the heading of common criminals for a firing squad. At least Carr could tell my family what had happened.

Hiram said, "We'll ditch the car about two blocks from the air base. Walter knows how to mess up the carburetor so it'll look as if we had to abandon it.

"There's a group of houses just outside the main gate of the field. The street is only a block long, from the highway we're on to the gate. There are twelve houses on each side. We want the fifth house from the highway on the south side. Have you got it?"

We said we understood. Hiram asked us to repeat what he'd said, and we did in turn. Then he asked us to see that our watches agreed.

"That's what they do in the comic strips," I said. "They're always synchronizing watches." Nobody thought it amusing. It's the kind of thing you say when your nerves are hopping.

Hiram said, "There are three doors to the house, front and back and one on the side away from the air base. I'll take the front door, Teensy the back, and Walter the side."

"What do I do?" I said.

If Hiram thought Maria was a prisoner inside that house, I wanted to go in.

"We've got to have a lookout, John." It was the first time he'd addressed me as anything but Mr. Stodder.

"You take the side nearest the air base. Get in the shadow of the next house. Can you whistle?"

I said I could, either straight or with two fingers.

"You don't have to be fancy," Hiram said with a grin. "If you see anyone heading for the house, whistle 'Dixie.' If they go past, stop whistling. If they come inside the grounds, whistle 'Reveille.' "

"What do I do then?" I said.

"Run like hell," Hiram said.

"May I ask who we are about to visit?"

"Major Felix Borodin," Hiram said, "although from what Papa Szabo said, the major won't be there to receive us. You see, he conducts a class in security at the air base during the next hour."

Hiram stopped the car and let Walter out. "Eight-five sharp," he said.

Teensy got out next. Hiram said, "Eight-five sharp," to her, too. She walked off into the shadows without a word.

I got out a block farther on. "Eight-five sharp," went for me as well. It was a clear, cold, starry night where a heavy snowstorm would have offered some concealment.

I had no trouble finding the street. I passed a couple of Russian soldiers off duty. I held my breath, but they never even glanced at me. It was hard walking on the uncleared sidewalks, and my feet still gave me excruciating pain, but I looked at my watch when I sighted the fifth house from the highway on the south side and I had two minutes' grace. The gun was still inside my jacket in the shoulder holster, but I could have handled it just as easily with boxing-gloves as with the bandages on my hands.

There wasn't a light in the house when I passed. There was no light in the next house, and, except for wading knee-deep in snow, I had no trouble in making my way across the lawn and into the shadows from the second house.

Major Felix Borodin's residence was no cracker-box affair. Such might be appropriate for Budapest commuters, but Russian officers required something more substantial. Borodin's, identical with the neighboring twenty-three, had two full stories and what appeared to be a spacious attic under a mansard roof. There was a cellar to be searched, too.

Eight-five became eight-ten, then eight-fifteen. The only sound came shortly after the appointed time when my ears caught the scraping noise of a window being opened an inch or two, so that I might be heard if I whistled. My three friends were apparently careful to draw the shades; at least, no light appeared.

When my watch told me it was nearly eight-twenty, I began to feel uneasy. It shouldn't have taken three veteran housebreakers fifteen minutes to find—my mind almost accepted the word body—to find Maria. The house wasn't that big. It couldn't be that they'd walked into a trap. One of the three would have cried out.

It took all my willpower to keep from moving. It was bitterly cold, my muscles were cramped and sore from the beating Schmidt had given me, but I didn't dare leave the shadows. It occurred to me that Hiram hadn't said what was to happen when they were ready to leave. Were we expected to meet at the car? We couldn't risk walking back together. How would I know when they left? If we didn't return to the car, how did we get back to Budapest? I cursed myself for not asking.

I think it was almost eight-thirty when I heard the plane take off. I know it was only a minute or two later that the two men appeared, coming from the direction of the air base.

I whistled "Dixie" as loud as I could. I'm sure they heard me inside.

When the two men turned in at Borodin's gate, I whistled "Reveille," but the plane was only a few hundred feet overhead, and the roar from its engines would have drowned a siren. By the time the noise from the air had subsided, the men were inside the house.

If I could have used my hands, I'd have fired a shot in the window. If there'd been a stone, I'd have thrown it to smash the glass.

I expected to hear shots, the sounds of a struggle, shouting. There was only silence except for the drone of the airplane engines in the distance. I expected more men from the air base, but none came. Perhaps they'd already entered, through the back door and the door on the other side, the way Teensy and Walter had gone in.

I waited five minutes, the longest five minutes I'd ever known. I couldn't make my nerves obey me longer.

I went to the window that had been opened. The drifted snow came almost to my waist. I put my ear to the opening and I could hear voices somewhere in the house but not in that room.

I managed to raise the window three feet or so, using my elbow as a lever, but I couldn't think how to remove the shade. I pulled on it with my elbow, thinking to rip it from the roller, but it snapped back and climbed the window with what seemed to me a monstrous screeching. I flattened myself against the wall next to the window, but nobody appeared.

The room was dark, but there was light in the hallway beyond.

I put one foot on the narrow ledge over the cellar window, intending to pull myself onto the windowsill with my elbows and into the room. But I stopped. What business did I have going into that house? I ought to be following Hiram's advice. I ought to run like hell. I couldn't handle the gun I was carrying. Once inside the house I'd be useless in a fight.

The proper course would be to seek help. But where? Who could I go to? The American legation couldn't and wouldn't interfere. When an intelligence agent is caught red-handed, his government disowns him. I didn't know any of the men who worked for Hiram. I couldn't go back to Papa Szabo even if I could have found Hiram's sedan, repaired the carburetor, made the engine start without keys, and then driven without the use of my hands. If anything was to be done to save Hiram, Teensy, and Walter I had to do it then.

All those considerations went through my mind in a few seconds that I paused in front of the open window. But I had to swing myself into that room in any case. I couldn't have fled without first knowing what had happened to Maria.

Chapter Seventeen
TRICK THAT FAILED

I stood just inside the window. I thought of closing it behind me but I decided it was smart to leave one possible avenue of escape.

The voices I had heard from outside were speaking Russian. Probably discussing what to do with Hiram, Teensy, and Walter. My knowledge of Russian is strictly limited, but I remembered some of the words from the G.I. handbook and I recognized "spy" and "enemy" and "shooting."

There was enough light from the hallway for me to cross the room without bumping into the furniture. When I reached the doorway, I realized the voices were coming from somewhere down the corridor, toward the rear of the house, on the same floor. I listened for that warm, low voice that I'd heard for the first time in compartment seven on the Orient Express. I tried to identify the voices of my three friends. But the speakers were Russians, without an accent.

They were the two men who had entered the house. They were doing all the talking.

I remembered Hiram's voice, the way he'd said, "Run like hell." There was no place for me to run to. I'd be picked up in five minutes if I tried to get back to Budapest where I had no friends. I even lacked an identity. Hiram had lifted my passport in the name of Jean Stodder, Swiss. He'd told me I was John Stodder, American, again, but the papers were in his pocket.

I put one foot into the hallway, and the floor creaked under me. I thought it loud as a pistol shot, but the voices droned on without a break. I crossed the hallway into the front room on the far side of the house.

There was only the dim light from the hallway. As soon as my eyes became adjusted, I found I was in what Europeans like to call the music room. There was a piano in one of the corners toward the back of the house and an old-fashioned overstuffed sofa in the other. Between the two pieces of furniture there were double doors, undoubtedly leading to the dining room. Light was streaming under them and through a slit in the center where they didn't quite meet. The voices were in that room and so were Hiram, Teensy, and Walter. I moved right up to the doors and I could see the three Americans sitting together on a sofa at right angles to me. I didn't see Maria. The Russians were out of my line of vision. They were still doing all the talking.

Had I been able to handle my gun, I could have surprised the Russians without difficulty. There was only one other possibility, to get my gun into the hands of my friends, tricking the Russians into dropping their guard for the moment.

I decided I'd have to draw them into the hallway, at the same time opening the double doors and kicking my gun along the floor to the sofa where one of the three Americans could quickly pick it up. I realized it was a slim chance.

I managed to drop my gun from its holster onto the sofa by bending over and hitting the bottom of the holster with my wrist. I found I could pick up the gun by using both my bandaged hands. I placed it carefully on the rug. I'd shove one of the double doors open with an elbow, then kick the gun with the opposite foot.

There was a large vase on the piano. I picked it up in my arms. I tiptoed to the door into the hallway. The Russians' voices seemed louder, as if the speakers were about to discard talk for action.

I measured the distance with my eye between the door into the hallway and the double doors into the dining room.

I raised my arms and tossed the heavy vase down the hallway, toward the other door to the dining room. I was a foot from the double doors when the vase landed with a crash that shook the house.

One of the double doors rolled back easily under the pressure from my elbow.

At the same time, I kicked the gun. It slid across the bare, polished floor. It stopped almost at Hiram Carr's feet.

In a split second, I had ducked under the piano. I expected one of the Russians to investigate the crash in the hallway, the other to fire where my head had been. The double diversion would give Hiram his chance to pick up the gun and use it.

But there was no shot, and I realized the door to the hallway hadn't opened.

That meant that my trick wasn't good enough, that the Russians hadn't left Hiram uncovered long enough for him to seize the gun at his feet.

Then someone moved. I heard his shoes scrape the bare floor and I saw his shadow move ahead of him through the doorway. The shadow moved to where I was crouching.

Then he spoke.

"Get up," Hiram Carr said. "Get up, John, and join us in the other room."

Chapter Eighteen
NEW STRATEGY

For a moment I was faint with relief. Then relief gave way to anger. No man likes to know he's made a fool of himself.

"Goddamit," I said, "how the hell was I supposed to know? Why didn't you say something? Why didn't someone come out and tell me?"

I was so let down and ashamed of myself and angry with Carr that I could only stare at him.

"I'm sorry," Hiram said. "It's my fault. I should have let you know. But I wanted you to stay out there in case we have any more visitors. That was a smart plan of yours just the same."

I was damned if I was going to be patronized by that birdlike little man with the pince-nez and the ridiculous coonskin cap on his grotesque head. But I noticed the two Russians seated against the wall and I shut my mouth. I could tell Hiram Carr what I thought of him sometime in the future—now that we had a future again.

It wasn't until I sat down on the sofa next to Walter that I noticed that Carr had a gun in his hand. The Russians were his prisoners all right; I guessed one of them had to be Major Felix Borodin. The other was a captain.

"Where is Maria Torres?" I said.

Carr shook his head. "She isn't here," he said. "There's no reason to believe she's ever been in this house."

"Do you know where she is?"

"I'm trying to get Major Borodin to tell us. He swears he doesn't know."

I was surprised to find that Hiram spoke fluent Russian. I suppose I was still thinking of him as the hick he'd pretended to be when Maria and I had met him in the dining car. Of course he wouldn't have received his assignment unless he'd known Russian.

When my temper had cooled, Hiram asked me to watch the street from inside the front door. He said something in Russian to Borodin, who nodded. Then Hiram told Walter that Borodin would go with him to get the car.

"He's going to ride back to Budapest with us," Hiram said. "He'll have to get us past the roadblocks."

"You told him you'd kill him if he didn't?"

"No," Hiram said, "but I've a stronger persuader than that. I told him I'd tell Lavrentiev about his connection with Doctor Schmidt."

"What about this other guy, the captain?"

"He doesn't know anything," Hiram said. "He's apparently one of Borodin's pupils in that security class. He says he came here with the major to get some books."

"What do we do with him?" I wasn't feeling very sore at Hiram any longer because the "we" slipped out naturally.

"Tie him and leave him," Hiram said. "Borodin can release him or whatever he plans to do when he gets back from Budapest."

"What do you mean 'or whatever he plans to do'?" I asked.

Hiram shrugged his shoulders. "It's none of our business," he said, "what Felix Borodin does with the captain. But he heard our conversation and he knows a lot of things about his instructor in security that Borodin would rather nobody knew."

When Walter returned with the car, he and Teensy hogtied the captain and stuck a gag in his mouth.

We were about to close the front door behind us when the telephone rang. Hiram hesitated a moment, then went back in the hallway and picked up the receiver. He listened, then beckoned to me. He held the receiver to my ear.

"Hello, hello, Felix?"

I'd have recognized that clipped, hard, and precise voice anywhere. I tried to disguise mine.

"Ja?" I said.

"You are late. Our engagement was for nine o'clock. I am very busy. Are you taking the next train?"

The doctor had been busy, all right. Busy enough to get away from Orlovska's before Lavrentiev's men arrived.

"Sehr gut," I said. "Ich kommt schnell."

"At the usual place, then, in thirty minutes."

"But where?" I asked Hiram when he'd replaced the receiver.

"Borodin will tell us, one way or another."

Hiram drove, and Teensy sat in front, with Borodin between them.

We hit the first roadblock on the outskirts of the city, near the race track. They waved us on when they saw the major's uniform. We had to produce identification to pass the police lines in front of the Keleti station, in spite of Borodin's presence. Hiram had satisfactory documents for all of us.

The gendarmery captain saluted. "Sorry," he said, "but it's orders from the MVD. Those foreigners who murdered the Russian Major Strakhov on the train."

"Any luck?" Hiram said.

"We'll catch them," the gendarmery captain said. "It takes time, that's all."

We drove toward the Danube, stopping in front of the Belvarosi coffeehouse, and Hiram went inside, coonskin cap and all. I suppose it was part of his front as the American agricultural attaché, the sort of costume Hungarians saw in Western movies and took to be typically American. I think Hiram figured nobody would believe flamboyant dress could hide an undercover operative.

When Hiram returned to the car, he told Borodin he could leave. The Russian went off without a word, his hands thrust deep into his pockets.

I thought Hiram had lost his mind to let Borodin go but I put it another way. I said, "Bet you a dollar he goes to Schmidt as fast as he can."

"No takers," Hiram said. "That's what I'm counting on."

"Did he tell you where they're meeting?"

"Of course not," Hiram said, "and I didn't bother to ask him because he would have lied. He's got to see Schmidt. Their only chance is to kill all four of us, now. Borodin's smart enough to know what would happen to him if Lavrentiev learns his connection with the German."

"So you calmly let him go free in the middle of Budapest," I said.

"I've got a man following him," Hiram said. "Why do you think I went into the Belvarosi?"

I still wasn't convinced. If Borodin was an instructor in security, he'd certainly be suspicious. And know how to duck Hiram's operative in short order. Our only chance to find Maria was through Dr. Schmidt. And Borodin was our only link with the German.

We hadn't been at Hiram's house fifteen minutes when the operative telephoned to say he'd lost Borodin. The Russian had pulled the ancient trick of boarding a crowded bus, getting on first because of his uniform, then ducking out the side door when the bus was about to start and Hiram's man was helplessly jammed inside.

"You said Schmidt and Borodin will figure they have to kill all four of us to keep us quiet," I said to Hiram. "What do we do? Wait around like sitting ducks? I don't see how we can find them now. We never should have let Borodin out of our sight."

"We haven't time to wait," Hiram said. "Come over to the window."

He drew aside the curtain. There were two men against the building across the street.

"We've had too much luck so far." I couldn't help

laughing, but he ignored it. "It can't last much longer. We've only a few hours left. We've got to find Marcel Blaye's envelope and get the hell out of Hungary."

"What about Maria Torres?"

Hiram put his hand on my shoulder. "I'm sorry," he said, "but there's nothing we can do. There isn't time. Schmidt knows where the envelope is. If you guessed by questioning Orlovska, the Russians can put two and two together and get the answer if they have time. We've got to move, John. We've got to get that envelope tonight."

"I'm not going to leave Maria," I said. "I can't do it. I went after Orlovska because you promised we'd find Maria. I took two hours of hell from Schmidt. I got you the answer you wanted. I found out where the envelope is. You haven't the right to let me down now."

"You're in love aren't you, John?"

"Of course I am," I said.

"How do you know Maria Torres didn't leave willingly with Schmidt? How do you know what her game is?"

"I know she didn't go of her own accord. There isn't any way for me to prove it. But I'm not going to leave her."

Hiram said, "But, John, I told you what possession of that Manila envelope means to Russia or the United States. It could mean the difference between war and peace. I'm an official of the United States Government, John. I haven't the right to risk the success of my mission for any individual. Believe me, I'm terribly sorry."

After a long pause, I said, "What can we do about the envelope? Jozsefvaros station must be crawling with armed Russians. We can't take over the way you did in Borodin's house. What's the plan?"

"I don't know," Hiram said. "All I know is that we've got to act in a hurry."

He took a large-scale map of Budapest from his desk and spread it on the floor.

"I'd suggest you get some rest. I'll ask Teensy to change those bandages on your hands."

When I left the room Hiram was down on all fours studying the map.

I went upstairs to the room I'd occupied briefly the night before and stretched out on the bed. I tried to sleep but there was nothing doing. Each time I closed my eyes I saw Maria's face.

I had come to Hungary to discover what had happened to my brother. I knew the answer. If I managed to stay alive a few more hours, I was due to leave without knowing what had happened to the girl I loved.

It seemed incredible Maria and I had been together only twenty-four hours, that little more than twice that time had passed since I boarded the Orient Express at the Westbahnhof in Vienna.

I remembered how Maria had looked the last time I had seen her. She'd turned to wave as she reached the door of the coffeehouse. Then Schmidt had opened the door as Otto, Hermann, and I were rounding the corner into the driving snow, and we heard the sobbing of the gypsy violins:

There's a Romany tale that up in the moon,
Each midnight a gypsy is playing a tune.
The melodies sweet from his fiddle that flow,
Are heard only by lovers as silent they go.
Then, my love, let us try while the moonlight is clear,
Amid the dark forest that fiddle to hear.

I recalled how my heart beat faster when I went back to the coffeehouse with Hiram and Teensy, how happy I'd been when we found Schmidt's car was still in front. For five minutes, until the Carrs came out, that had meant reunion with Maria.

Teensy had broken the news. She'd said, "I'm afraid there's a hitch. Your girl isn't there. The proprietor said she and Schmidt left an hour ago."

How had the German doctor forced Maria to leave the coffeehouse? She'd told me, "Hurry back, I'll be waiting." I would never believe she went of her own free will. On the other hand, he wouldn't have risked threatening her with a gun in that crowded place.

And why had he abandoned his car? Not to mislead us. He hadn't known I was coming back. Just the opposite. He was sure Otto and Hermann would follow his instructions to kill me in the Keleti yards after I found the envelope.

The doctor might have left his car if he'd held up the coffeehouse, if he'd forced the proprietor and the patrons to stand by while he took Maria away at gun point. He wouldn't have trusted the car to start immediately with a crowd pursuing him. It would be easier to shake them off by heading into the storm.

But if that had been the case, Schmidt wouldn't have come back for the car. The proprietor would have called the police, who would have taken it. Yet Schmidt or one of his men had returned for it, or at least I assumed that was the car whose tires Hiram had slashed when they rescued me from Orlovska's.

The proprietor had told Teensy and Hiram that the German and Maria departed shortly after I had gone to the yards, nearly an hour before my return. He hadn't said anything about Schmidt using force. And that would have been a major event in the life of a coffee-house keeper.

None of these hypotheses made sense. There had to be another answer.

I'd told Teensy when she broke the news, "You didn't look far enough. The proprietor's a liar."

The next thing I realized, I was going down the stairs two steps at a time. I nearly broke down the door into Hiram's study.

"The proprietor *was* a liar," I shouted at the startled Hiram. "That's the answer. Can't you see?"

The intelligence agent looked at me as if he thought I'd lost my mind. He scrambled to his feet. Teensy came running from the other room.

"Take it easy, take it easy," Teensy said.

"Easy nothing," I said. "That's the answer. Schmidt never took Maria out of the coffeehouse. His car was still there because *he* was still there. Don't you see it?"

Hiram fixed me a Scotch and soda.

"We've been so busy we haven't had time to think," I said. I took half the drink at one gulp. I told Hiram and Teensy what had been running through my mind before I leaped from the bed like a jack-in-the-box.

"Schmidt wouldn't have waited in just any coffeehouse," I said. "He's in just as much trouble with the authorities as we are. He has to be even more careful because he hasn't diplomatic plates on his car. He wouldn't have picked the coffeehouse he did unless he had good reason. Ordinarily, he would have been afraid of being recognized by the train crews who go there. They would certainly have remembered a beauty like Maria.

"The doctor went there for only one reason. Because the proprietor was a member of the gang. Because he could be trusted to lie to anyone asking questions.

"Maria is still there. I'll stake my life on it."

"You're going to," Hiram said. He took off his pince-nez and rubbed his nose. "What was it Schmidt said on the telephone at Borodin's?"

"What's that got to do with it?" I said.

"A lot. What did he say?"

"Well, he said Borodin was late and I said yes. He asked if Borodin was taking the next train and I said yes again. Then he said he'd see him at the usual place in thirty minutes."

Hiram took a copy of the Hungarian railway guide from the bookshelf.

"The train that Borodin would have caught gets to Keleti in twenty-two minutes. It's about five minutes from his house to the station. That means that the 'usual place' Schmidt mentioned is three minutes from Keleti."

"That would fit our coffeehouse," I said. "It's worth trying. Will you try it?"

"I've got business with Herr Doktor Schmidt," Hiram said. "We've got to try the railway car at Jozsefvaros to-night." He rubbed his chin. "It would help if we could eliminate any possible competition from Schmidt before we start."

Chapter Nineteen
THE BODY IN THE CELLAR

The two men were still across the street when Hiram, Teensy, Walter, and I drove off. They made no move to follow.

"They won't arrest me yet," Hiram said. "They'd rather wait to catch me red-handed. Then they'll stage the biggest trial you ever saw." He spoke without emotion, as if he were discussing a bridge tournament or a birthday party. He had no nerves.

I felt an urge to keep the conversation going.

"Why do you suppose Borodin, a major in the Russian Army, got mixed up with Schmidt?"

"Why do any of them sell out?" Hiram said. "Usually it's money or women or both. Sometimes it's ambition, sometimes wounded vanity.

"Marcel Blaye fell for Orlovska. He wanted to go back to Germany, and the Russians promised him a high post in their East German government.

"Look at Orlovska. She wants money and luxury. She'll sell out to anybody to get an easy life. But in this racket, the Blayes, the Orlovskas, and the Borodins don't last too long. Traitors and double-dealers usually hang themselves. Men like Schmidt are the tough ones.

They're dedicated fanatics, men with one idea that dominates their lives. You can't buy them or convert them or curb them. In a normal world, Blaye, Orlovska, and Borodin would probably be in jail but Schmidt would be confined to an insane asylum."

We drove past the coffeehouse. There were two stories above the café. The roof was flat. There was an alley on one side, separating the coffeehouse from the shop of a stonecutter whose sign announced he made tombstones for the Kerepesitemetö, the huge municipal cemetery across the street. There was a four-story tenement against the other wall of the coffeehouse.

We swung round the block, and the illuminated clock in the Keleti station tower said the time was ten thirty-five. It was more than an hour since we'd dropped Major Felix Borodin. Considering the time required to shake Hiram's operative, Borodin had met Schmidt in the coffeehouse a good half hour earlier.

We couldn't see the rear of the coffeehouse because of the surrounding buildings. Hiram said it was probable there was an open space behind, to which the alley led.

When we had made almost a full circle, Walter and I dropped off. We would go inside the café. Teensy and Hiram would be outside, to cover our exit in case of trouble. The proprietor had never seen either Walter or me but he would remember the Carrs as having inquired about Maria and Schmidt. The car would be parked on the far side of the cemetery, an area of warehouses deserted at night.

Teensy had changed the bandages on my hands for skimpier dressings, and I was sure I could handle a gun, although with a good deal of pain. At any rate, I carried the Luger in the shoulder holster.

We stood just inside the door for a moment. I took a quick look but I saw neither Schmidt nor Borodin. There weren't more than twenty-five or thirty patrons, seated at small tables. The headwaiter beckoned to us to take a table near the gypsy band which was on a platform, but I shook my head, and we sat near the door. As soon as we had ordered, I took a couple of newspapers from the rack so that we could hide our faces if we had to. We drank our coffee and pretended to read. It didn't help any that I'd picked papers in Turkish and Greek, of which neither Walter nor I understood a word.

After a couple of coffees, I called the waiter and asked him in German for the men's room. He sent me through a doorway in the corner back of the gypsies' platform. The men's room was at the end of a thirty-foot corridor. The stairway to the second floor was off the corridor, about halfway down.

There was a dim gaslight at the head of the stairs, but there was enough light for me to see two doors which were numbered. At first I thought it might be smart to engage a room. But we had no baggage. It was the kind of place where a couple could get a room without baggage but a man alone would be looked upon with suspicion.

I went back to the table, and Walter went through the same routine.

Most of the men in the coffeehouse were from the railroad yards. There were two or three Wagons-Lits porters in their brown uniforms, trainmen in the habitual dark blue, and enginemen whose calling was apparent, even in civilian clothes, from the coal-dust tinge of their skins. The few women seemed to be there for the ancient purpose.

There was a short, barrel-chested man who moved through the room conversing with the customers. I took him to be the proprietor. I'd forgotten to ask Hiram to describe him. The finger-marked menu on the table said the owner's name was Georgy Kis, but his Prussian mustache and bristly haircut made me think he'd been born Georg Klein and later Magyarized his name.

By the time Walter returned, I had decided I was going to climb the stairs. After another coffee, I'd tell Walter within the waiter's hearing that I felt ill. I'd make sure I looked ill, too, on my way to the corridor. I didn't think it would take me long to case the upstairs floors, but if Walter found the need to warn me, he was to give the gypsies five dollars to play "Lilli Marlene," a tune every band in Central Europe knows by heart.

The corridor was empty, and I made the second floor without being seen. I thought the stairs creaked unduly under the tattered red carpet, but the gypsy band was attacking "Black Eyes" with gusto sufficient to cover anything.

There were half a dozen rooms on the second floor. The doors were closed, and there was no way to tell which were occupied without hearing voices. I stood at the end of the narrow hallway, as far from the flickering gaslight as possible, until the music stopped. Someone was talking in the third room. I put my ear to the door but a man was speaking Hungarian without an accent, an ability which neither Schmidt nor Borodin possessed.

I tried the top floor. I heard a woman scream and I raced down the corridor, but when I reached the door she was shouting in Hungarian. I went downstairs as fast as I could.

The proprietor was talking with Walter in German when I returned to the table. He turned to bow to me. I tried to read his face, but it was totally without expression.

"May I suggest a Fernet Branca?" he said. "I find an upset stomach nearly always comes from one's nerves." He glanced at my bandaged hands.

"Something I ate," I said. "My nerves are fine."

When the music started again and the proprietor had moved away, I buried my nose in the Athens paper and tried to figure the next move.

I couldn't shuttle between the café and the upper floors indefinitely. I'd been lucky to get away with one visit without being caught. There was no way to determine behind which of the twelve doors Schmidt and Borodin might be conferring, if they were in the place at all. I couldn't try all the doors or break down the locked ones to see if Maria were a prisoner in one of them.

The only course was to drink coffee and pretend to read and hope that Schmidt or Borodin would appear. I put down the paper and started to explain to Walter, but it wasn't necessary because Schmidt came in the front door at that moment. Borodin was not with him.

I kicked Walter under the table. I held the newspaper in front of my face, but I was placed so that I could watch Schmidt out of the corner of my eye. I expected him to head for the corridor which led to the stairway but he stood just inside the door. He stuck his head forward like a vulture, peering through those gold-rimmed spectacles until he spotted the proprietor and went to him at the far end of the room. They talked for some time, their bullet heads close together. I got the impression that Schmidt was excited; he used his hands steadily in emphasis.

I called our waiter and paid the bill. I wanted to be ready to leave the moment Schmidt did. He wore no hat or coat, and I guessed he couldn't have come far, that he'd left his things in some nearby building.

The proprietor accompanied Schmidt to the door, and they shook hands.

I didn't want to risk bumping into Schmidt in front of the place so I counted to sixty before Walter and I got up from the table and followed. We reached the sidewalk just in time to see him enter the tenement next door.

"We've got to tell the Carrs," I said to Walter. "You watch to see Schmidt doesn't come out again. I'll try to find Hiram in the alley."

"Whistle 'Dixie,' Mr. Stodder," Walter said. "That's our signal. Seems only Americans know that tune."

I waded through the snow to the back of the alley, praying that Hiram wouldn't put a bullet through my head before I could come near enough to risk whistling.

I took cover behind a large block of granite, on the edge of the stonecutter's property. I stuck my head out and whistled the first few bars of "Dixie." I listened but nobody came and there was no response. I waited a minute or so and then whistled louder, but still nothing happened. I moved across the alley, into the yard back of the coffeehouse. I whistled again and still there was no answer.

I went back to the sidewalk, to Walter.

"They don't answer," I said. I thought I might have misunderstood Hiram's plan, but Walter confirmed it. Teensy and Hiram would be outside to cover our exit in case of trouble.

"Maybe they're across the street," Walter said. But we both knew that was impossible. There was only a thin strip of sidewalk in front of the high iron fence which keeps the living out of the cemetery. There wasn't any place, other than the alley and the back yard, from which Hiram and Teensy could have watched the coffeehouse.

We couldn't stand on the sidewalk indefinitely.

"I guess we'd better follow Schmidt," Walter said. "Maybe Mr. and Mrs. Carr went around the corner for a cup of coffee. It's cold standing in the snow."

That was no moment to start thinking of what might have happened.

We went into the four-story tenement. There weren't any letterboxes with names on them. It didn't matter, though, because the cellar door was ajar, and we heard

voices and we knew what had happened to Hiram and
Teensy.

We found them at the foot of the cellar stairs. The
body of Major Felix Borodin was lying twenty feet away,
half concealed by the furnace. The door at the far end
of the cellar was opened, the wooden door banging
back and forth in the wind.

"Schmidt killed him," Hiram said.

I went to the back door and there was enough light
to see tracks in the fresh snow.

"When Schmidt left here to go to the coffeehouse,"
Teensy said, "we spotted him. We knew he was coming
back because he'd left his hat and coat. We figured we
could look over the place while he was next door.

"We heard him come back, but he didn't come upstairs as we'd counted. By the time Hiram got down
here, Schmidt had fired two shots. Then he must have
heard Hiram's step on the stairs because he went
through the door over there."

First Marcel Blaye, then Ivan Strakhov, now Felix
Borodin.

"You'd better go upstairs," Hiram said quietly. "Up
on the top floor."

I didn't have to ask what he meant.

"Schmidt was on his way up there," Hiram said.
"That was next."

"There's nobody else in the building," Teensy said.
"You can go right up."

I had to call Walter to help me break down the door
because Schmidt had locked it from the outside. I heard
muffled sounds through the door, the same sounds that

must have told Hiram and Teensy who was locked up inside.

I stood on the threshold. I was afraid to walk in. I was afraid of what I might see. I called her name, and she staggered toward me. I caught her in my arms.

I knew then that I would kill Dr. Schmidt if it took me the rest of my life to find him.

Chapter Twenty
PERILOUS PLANS

Two men in a car followed us back to Hiram's house. They stayed only a hundred feet or so behind after picking us up where Hiram had left his sedan, on the far side of the cemetery. The men we'd spotted across the street from the house were still there, only now there were three instead of two.

It wasn't pleasant to realize they'd known what was happening from the start. They'd deliberately allowed Schmidt and the Americans to carry on a finish fight. It had cost them nothing. They were serving notice on us that the final round had started in the battle for Marcel Blaye's Manila envelope.

The sudden knowledge of what the Russian game had been explained a good many things. It explained why I hadn't been picked up in the Arizona, why Hermann and Otto had been permitted to reach Budapest as deserters from the Red Army in a stolen army car. It explained why Hiram's activities hadn't been curbed and why Schmidt had been allowed to move around at will. It explained Major Felix Borodin who'd done a very neat job of counterintelligence—until Schmidt had caught him at it.

It also explained the fact that Hiram, Teensy, Walter, Maria, and I were still at liberty. The Russians knew everything but the location of the envelope. We'd remain free until we led them to it or Schmidt did.

But for the moment, the only thing that mattered was to get a doctor for Maria. I tried to get Hiram to stop at a doctor's office or the hospital, but he said it was too dangerous, that the hospital would hold Maria for several days. They would call the police as soon as we brought her in.

As it was, the Russians saw us carry her to the car and they saw us take her into Hiram's house. To them it was another detail which concerned only Schmidt and us.

She was hysterical when I found her. I didn't have to ask a question to know the whole story. Some of Schmidt's instruments were on the bureau.

Teensy put her to bed in the guest room. Hiram finally managed to get a doctor after calling half a dozen; it was after midnight, and he couldn't explain on the phone. I was afraid she might be scarred for life, but the doctor said he didn't think so. He said she should have absolute tranquility, that she ought to go away for a long rest. I thought of what lay ahead of us that night and thanked him.

As soon as Maria was asleep, I joined Hiram in his study. He had spread the map of Budapest on the floor. When I entered the room, he was squatting in front of the fireplace, feeding papers to the flames. It meant that when we left the house that night, it was for good.

Hiram was burning his confidential documents and his codes.

"What are you going to do about Maria?" I said. "We can't move her. She's in no condition to travel."

"Teensy and Millie will take her to that inn in the Buda hills. They'll be among friends."

I was about to ask how they'd get past the roadblock but I realized then that the Russians had set up road-blocks in order to keep a check on our movements and those of Schmidt, not to stop us. We'd pass roadblocks all right until the MVD had Blaye's Manila envelope in their hands.

Hiram rubbed his hand across his forehead. I knew how tired he must be. I don't think he'd had an hour's sleep in two days.

"Why don't you go with them?" he said. "Walter and I can take care of the business at Jozsefvaros."

A few hours earlier I might have agreed. I had told myself I had no interest in Blaye's envelope. That was before Hiram had revealed its importance, but, never-theless, I had tried to make a bargain with Schmidt. I had been willing to give him the envelope in return for Maria's safety and my freedom to carry out the mission that had brought me to Hungary on a murdered man's passport. But that was before I learned my brother's fate from the bitch who had betrayed him. It was be-fore Schmidt had "entertained" me at Orlovska's. It was before I had stood in the doorway of that room in the tenement and seen what Schmidt had done to the woman I loved.

"You go to hell," I said to Hiram. "I'm in this to stay."

"You mustn't worry about Maria," he said. "Come look at this map, and I'll tell you why."

He pointed to the location of the country inn. Then he moved his finger about a mile to the west.

"There's a dirt road about a hundred yards north of the inn. A little over a mile down that road there's a long stretch of flat, open field."

He glanced at his watch.

"Exactly at dawn, in slightly more than five and a half hours, a United States Air Force plane will land in that field. It will take off with Maria, Millie, and Teensy aboard. I hope it will take off with Marcel Blaye's envelope. I think it possible that either you or Walter or I will be alive at dawn, at seven forty-four."

It was on the tip of my tongue to tell him that I might deliver the envelope to the plane but that I wasn't leaving Hungary until I'd had a final settlement with Schmidt. It occurred to me, though, that I would be insulting him by assuming I'd be the one still alive in five and a half hours.

Hiram called Walter into the room, and we located Jozsefvaros freight station on the map. We couldn't get away from the cemetery. Where Keleti station, the coffeehouse, and the tenement were on the northern edge of the burying ground, Jozsefvaros bordered it on the south. The layout resembled a huge letter D with Keleti at the top, Jozsefvaros at the bottom, and the curving part the connecting tracks. The cemetery took up most of the inside, and the vertical line represented Fiumei ut, one of the city's main thoroughfares.

The freight station and the yards paralleled the cemetery's length of four city blocks. The station took up a quarter of that distance, with six loading platforms on as many tracks.

I noticed something else. Right where the tracks entered the station, there was a large building, the army barracks which houses the Budapest garrison.

Hiram nodded. "And something the map doesn't show," he said, "is that the station is surrounded by a high stone wall. The only way to enter uninvited is to walk the tracks from a point well outside the yards."

I went upstairs to say goodbye to Maria. I knocked but there was no answer. The door was unlocked, and I went in to find her sleeping soundly, the raven-black hair framing her lovely dark face against the white of the pillow.

I bent over and kissed her forehead. I started out the door and then, because the book says you keep a sense of humor in such cases, I took Ilonka's charm against the evil eye from my pocket and laid it on Maria's pillow next to her head.

Chapter Twenty-One
RUNAWAY LOCOMOTIVE

The car that followed us to Hiram's trailed us again when we left the house for the last time.

We had decided to separate in order to shake them. After dropping me near the Danube Corso, Hiram would drive Walter to Buda, then return to Pest to abandon the car. We agreed to meet at three o'clock near the railway tracks, a quarter mile from the Jozsef-varos yards.

Hiram had said the chances were that one of us would come out of the yards. There would be a car in an alley at 188 Asztalos Sandor ut which borders the tracks from Keleti to Jozsefvaros and was close by our three-o'clock meeting-place. Hiram estimated forty minutes to reach the makeshift flying-field, which meant that whichever of us got to the car would have to get there by seven o'clock.

I found before leaving the house that I could handle a gun, although with some difficulty and at the risk of opening the wounds on my hands. Each of us carried two ammunition clips for our Lugers. With one cart-ridge already in each chamber, that gave us seventeen shots apiece, which Hiram suggested should be enough to take over the city.

When I left the car it was the first time I'd been alone and on foot in the center of Budapest in more than nine years. I found myself in front of the old redoubt. Across the square and facing the Danube had been the Hangli Gardens, traditional afternoon drinking spot for American and British newspapermen. Now the Hangli was gone. In its place was a tall stone shaft with a tiny stone airplane on top, Russia's memorial to her pilots who died in the city's capture from the Nazis. The square had been renamed in honor of Molotov.

I walked through the Vaci utca, a glittering shopping center before the war. The old familiar names were on the stores but nearly every one bore the sign *Nationalized*, and the show windows were bare.

There were pictures of Generalissimo Stalin everywhere. It gave me the chills to see the mustachioed dictator's face side by side with the yellow posters inviting my capture.

I walked past the Belvarosi coffeehouse, and the gypsy band was playing the melody that reminded me of Maria just when I wanted to forget how much she had come to mean to me. I knew what lay ahead and how little chance there was that I should ever see her again.

Then, my love, let us try while the moonlight is clear,
Amid the dark forest that fiddle to hear.

I won't pretend my nerves were calm. I fancied I saw an MVD agent in every man and woman I passed. It was the same on the bus; each new passenger seemed vaguely familiar. I'd seen their faces before. I sat in the back of the bus; I expected at any moment to feel a gun in my ribs.

There was one heavyset man I was sure had been on the train to Budapest. He left the bus behind me; for two blocks the crunching of heavy footsteps in the snow told me I was being followed.

I checked an impulse to run. Instead, I turned into a side street, off the avenue that would take me to Hiram and Walter. The footsteps were louder than ever.

The night was bitter cold and clear. The moon had not yet risen, but there was sufficient light from the stars to tell me, when there was no possibility of turning back, that I had entered a dead-end street.

Three chimneys standing against the sky at the end of the street meant three houses wall to wall in front of me. There was no alley, no passage for further retreat.

There was a short stretch of sidewalk cleared by the wind. Before my feet hit the snow again I heard the relentless pounding behind me.

The three houses at the end of the street were dark. They could be apartments with unlocked front doors. They could be private houses, ending my flight on the doorstep.

I passed the first house. If I reached for my gun with my bandaged hands, I'd get a bullet in my back. The footsteps, echoing against the buildings from the hard-packed snow, were scarcely ten feet behind.

I passed the second house, and the door of the third house opened under my hand. I stepped inside and

pulled the door behind me. I was in the hallway of a
tenement, like the one in which we'd found Maria.
There was a dim night light.

I'd taken several steps toward the stairs when I heard
the door opening. I turned and flattened myself against
the wall, in back of the door.

The door swung open very slowly, so slowly that I
managed to get out my gun. I held it by the barrel and
when the head appeared I brought down the butt of
the gun as hard as I could. He sank to the floor with a
crash and lay still.

I pulled him over to the wall, then ran through his
pockets. I expected to find a gun, but there wasn't one.
There was only a broken bottle in the back pocket, the
apricot brandy soaking his clothing and running in a
little trickle across the bare wooden floor.

Then I heard a door open somewhere upstairs and
a woman's voice said, "Jeno, Jeno. Is that you?" When
there was no answer, there were footsteps descending
the stairs and the woman said, "Drunk again."

I think I must have run through the snow all the way
back to the main avenue, then the three blocks to the
meeting place.

We started down the tracks toward Jozsefvaros after
Hiram had cut away the bandage from the fingers of
my right hand so that I could use my gun.

For most of the distance there was a stone wall to
cut off the tracks from the street, but here and there
it had crumbled under bombardment or shellfire, and
we entered on the right of way through one of those

holes. We went single file with Hiram leading, Walter
next, and me bringing up the rear, sixty or seventy feet
apart.

Hiram's plan was for Walter and me to wait at the
entrance to the station while he located the Austrian
coach and discovered how it was guarded. He would
rejoin us and sketch out a plan of attack. It would have
been a good deal easier if I could have told him at
which end of the car I had hidden Blaye's Manila envelope.

There was just enough light to pick our way slowly
along the ties. I couldn't help thinking that I'd entered
Hungary by walking the tracks and now I was finishing
the nightmare in the same fashion. Only I no longer
had the slightest illusion about the possibility of escape.
In the unlikely event that I lived through the next hour,
there was still Dr. Schmidt.

We had about a quarter of a mile to walk to the
yards, then three city blocks to the station. A hundred
yards or so short of the yards there were two big locomotives under a water tower. As far as I could tell, there
was no one aboard although they had steam up. I
thought they must have been scheduled to pull early-
morning trains out of Keleti station, probably including
the Vienna local. Fortunately, their headlights were not
switched on, or the rest of our walk would have been
on a brightly illuminated stage.

I caught up with Walter at the entrance to the yards,
in the shadow of the army barracks, which stood a few
feet from the tracks on our left. Except for a dim light

on each floor of the big building, the red and green signals, and the faint light from the hooded switches, we were shielded by darkness.

We stood without speaking for what seemed an hour although it couldn't have been more than ten minutes at the most. I wanted a cigarette desperately but I didn't dare light a match.

Hiram said the Austrian passenger car was on the innermost of the six tracks, to our right as we faced the station. To the left of the car there was a loading platform. To the right was a stone wall, then a narrow street, and the cemetery.

"There are two guards with tommy guns on the platform," Hiram said. "There's another on the back platform. There's a light inside so there may be others."

"Can we get in back of them?" I said.

"There isn't a chance," Hiram said. "There isn't a three-inch clearance between the car and the wall."

"What about the other tracks?" I said. "What about the track on the other side of the same platform?"

"Solid with boxcars. All the other tracks are filled."

"Can't we go along the top of the freight cars?" I said. "We could get to the back of the platform that way."

"No," Hiram said. "The roofs of the loading platform sheds extend over the tracks. There's no clearance for a man to walk on top of the cars. We couldn't even crawl."

"How about going under them?" Walter said.

"Too much snow," Hiram said.

"What's left?"

"We'll have to scale the wall in back of the platforms," Hiram said.

That meant retracing our steps to the place where
we had met and leaving the tracks to walk the streets to
Fiumei ut, which paralleled the sidewalk in back of the
platforms.

We started back the way we'd come, only I led and
Hiram came last.

The whole business made no sense to me. Hiram
should have known what we would be up against before
we started. There must have been some way to find out.

Hiram had said the stone wall around the Jozsefvaros
station was ten or twelve feet high. We couldn't hope to
scale a blank wall without a ladder or some other help.
And even if we could find such an aid, a thousand to
one shot, how could we hope to use it on the Fiumei ut,
one of the main streets of Budapest and pretty well
traveled even at three-thirty in the morning? I remembered it as a well-lighted street, but it was sufficiently
policed to make suicide any such operation as Hiram
contemplated, even if the lights were dim.

Then, too, the map had shown a large open space
between the loading platforms and the Fiumei ut wall,
including a driveway for trucks to deliver shipments to
the platforms. If we succeeded in reaching the top of
the wall, we'd have to drop twelve feet into that open
space, then cross the driveway to the shelter of the
platforms. We might not be watched but we wouldn't
know until we hit the top of the wall and then it might
be too late.

There had to be some other way to get into the Austrian car to retrieve Marcel Blaye's envelope. Hiram's idea of approaching from the yards was sound. What we needed was a diversion to draw the attention of the guards, something to take them away from the passenger car for just enough time to allow our search.

Perhaps one of us could fire a gun out in the yards? The guards would rush to investigate. But I knew that wasn't any good because it would then be impossible to leave by the tracks, the only exit Hiram had found because of that stone wall.

I think all three of us must have thought of the locomotive at the same time. At any rate, we all tried to talk at once when I went back to Walter and Hiram caught up with us.

We sneaked up alongside the locomotives, and they were deserted. We checked the switches and they were set straight into one of the middle tracks on which three flimsy wooden boxcars were standing at a loading platform.

I mounted to the cab of the locomotive nearest the yards. I gave Hiram and Walter three minutes by my watch to move as close as possible to the Austrian coach. Then I released the brakes, pulled the throttle wide, and jumped as the big machine began to roll.

I fell into a snowbank alongside the track. I picked myself up and ran after the locomotive as fast as I dared in the semidarkness but I was a good hundred yards from the Austrian coach when the engine plowed into the wooden boxcars.

There was a crash that must have been heard a mile. Then the engine jumped the tracks, sideswiped the

loading platform and toppled on its side with a great
roar of steam. I reached the passenger car, three tracks
away, as the boiler blew up, scattering hunks of those
matchbox freight cars like rain.

I was in time to boost Hiram over the coupling onto
the back platform of the car. Walter had apparently
climbed up before him. There was no sign of Walter
nor of any guards. They had rushed over to the track
where the locomotive struck.

In the next minute, all of Jozsefvaros went crazy. A
siren screamed, whistles blew, a bugle echoed from the
roof of the army barracks, the sounds accompanied by
the hissing of steam from the wrecked locomotive.

Hiram and Walter returned to the back platform.
Walter reached the ground first, and I knew by the way
he gripped my shoulder that they had found the Manila
envelope.

Walter reached out to help Hiram down.

At that moment, the floodlights went on.

We were shielded by the freight cars on the next
track, between us and the station offices and the barracks. But our escape route over the tracks, back to the
spot where we had left the street, was blocked. The arcs
lit up the station and the yards like a baseball stadium
at night.

We climbed onto the car platform and hurried
through the corridor to the other end. The large space
between the backs of the loading platforms and the
high stone wall was in half-darkness, illuminated faintly
by the light from the yards.

There was a door in the wall, a high wooden door,

in the corner nearest the cemetery. We couldn't have entered that way because the lock was on the inside, but it offered our only chance to get out.

The door in the wall was about a hundred feet from where we stood on the rear platform of the Austrian coach. For most of the distance there were two or three feet of snow. There was no time to lose. The guards who had hurried to the other platform when the loco-motive crashed would be back any second.

We walked off the coach onto the platform, then jumped into the snow and waded as fast as we could through the drifts toward the door in the high stone wall. Walter was ahead of me, Hiram behind.

When I caught up with Walter in front of the door, I saw he was trying to pull back the heavy brass bolt. The door would open in, and snow was drifted against it. Hiram and I worked feverishly to clear it away but it was slow going with only our hands as scoops.

Walter got the bolt back and we had cleared enough snow so that the door would open two or three feet, enough for us to slip through.

None of us realized the significance of the thin iron pipe that ran along the wall just above the door. We never noticed it in the half-light until it was too late. You see, the moment Walter started to swing that heavy door, the electrical connection broke and set off an alarm in the station. We couldn't hear the alarm, which meant we had no warning. We tugged at that big door until the searchlight went on, and then there was no place to hide.

I suppose the alarm went off when anything happened anywhere along that long stretch of wall. The searchlight stabbed back and forth for a few seconds before it came to rest on us, huddled in front of that door. Walter found it on the station roof but there was a burst of shots from a tommy gun before he fired into the searchlight and put it out of commission. The gunner on the roof must have had buck fever because only one bullet took effect. That one plowed into Hiram, and he crumpled without a sound.

There was no telling how much longer we'd have the darkness. There could be another searchlight. At any rate, they'd come after us quick enough. We might have heard shouts if the siren hadn't resumed its hysterical wailing.

We left Hiram where he'd fallen and pulled desperately at the door. I found I could slip through, but Walter was a lot bigger, and it took a minute or so to give him enough space to pass, dragging Hiram.

By that time, the siren had trailed off into a low moan, and we could hear the voices of the sentries moving across the loading yard toward the door and us. There was no way to pull the door shut behind us; there was no hardware, no handle on the outer side.

I told Walter to get Hiram to the car. I'd try to hold off the guards until he could get a head start. They'd have a chance on the street that paralleled the cemetery. It wasn't much used, even in the daytime.

Walter took Hiram in his arms like a baby. It was more than half a mile to the car on the Asztalos Sandor ut.

They were swallowed up in the darkness even before I moved to the right of the door. I flattened myself against the wall with my right arm and my gun straight out from the shoulder. It occurred to me they might come over the wall instead of through the door but in that case they'd need to go back for a ladder and that would give Walter and Hiram precious tune.

But they came straight to the door. I heard the Russian voices. A flashlight probed the opening. When the arm came through, I fired. I hit it, too, because there was a yell of pain and a lot of violent cursing from the arm and his companions. The hit was dumb luck; my finger was so smashed that I had to pull the trigger instead of squeezing it and the gun jumped in my hand.

For a minute or so there was no sound from behind the door. I was counting the seconds to myself, trying to imagine how far Walter had progressed with the unconscious Hiram, how long to wait, if I had the choice, before making a break. Not that I was going to follow them once they reached the car. I might help to get them there—but I was going to the warehouse on Mexikoi ut in search of Herr Doktor Schmidt.

The flashlight stabbed through the doorway once more, and then they pulled the hoary trick of shoving out a uniform cap on the end of a bayonet. But I fired at that, and it quickly withdrew behind the wall, and there was dead silence again.

When I had counted almost to a hundred, I was sure they'd gone for the ladder.

I left the wall, crossed the narrow street to the sidewalk bordering the iron fence, and moved warily in the direction which Walter had taken. I had to cross directly in front of the door. I made it, either because the Russians were keeping well back from the opening or because I was shrouded in the shadows from the tombs on the other side of the fence.

I crossed the street again and followed Walter's tracks by the reflected light from the arcs in the yards. I managed to keep up a sort of half-running, half-walking pace. I wondered how soon I'd run into a Russian patrol.

Two blocks and there was a low, open shed against the wall of the yards. I wasn't more than a few feet away when I heard Walter's voice. I hurried forward because I thought he must be talking to Hiram and the latter had regained consciousness. Walter must have put Hiram down in the shelter of the shed to look after the wound.

I was almost on top of them when I heard another voice, and it wasn't Hiram's.

It was the voice of Dr. Schmidt.

Chapter Twenty-Two
BLOOD ON THE SNOW

I stood where I was. When Schmidt came out of the shed and his body and the gun in his hand were outlined against the sky, I had plenty of time to aim. I held the Luger with both hands to steady my aim and I managed to squeeze the trigger as if I were squeezing a lemon. I should have emptied the eight bullets into his ugly body. But nothing happened.

My gun was jammed.

I saw Schmidt back off the sidewalk into the street as if it were all a dream. I watched him until I couldn't see him any longer in the inky blackness along the cemetery fence on the other side of that narrow street.

I walked up to where Walter was standing. I could make out Hiram's body stretched on the floor of the shed.

I didn't have to ask whether Schmidt had Marcel Blaye's Manila envelope. He wouldn't have left without it. He'd surprised Walter with Hiram in his arms. Walter never had a chance to draw his gun. I supposed he hadn't killed them because he didn't want to advertise his presence to the Russians. He must have known all the time what we were up to in the yards. We'd done his dirty work for him.

I bent over Hiram, and he was still breathing. I took his gun from his pocket and aimed it at the end of the shed, and it fired okay. I left my jammed Luger with him.

I told Walter to keep on going with Hiram, to get him to the car. My watch said it was five minutes after six. Walter was to give Hiram first aid in the car. If I didn't arrive by seven o'clock, he was to head for the Buda hills without me.

I crossed the street again, this time following Schmidt's footprints in the snow.

The moon had been up half an hour or so, but there were heavy snow clouds in the sky, and the light from the moon was fitful. I knew that street afforded no exit for another two blocks. There was the high stone wall of the railway yards on one side and the cemetery fence on the other. Schmidt would hurry but he wouldn't know I was behind him. I had to catch him in those two blocks, before he reached the main avenue where he'd have a car.

Every now and then the clouds would scud from in front of the moon, and I checked his tracks in the snow. The snow was fresh, and the street was infrequently used; those who were forced to travel it at night shunned the sidewalk that touched the cemetery. Schmidt's were the only marks in the snow. They were easy to follow when there was light. There wasn't a street lamp in sight or I should have spotted him when he passed them a block or even two ahead.

I was nearly at the end of the street and beginning to think I'd lost Schmidt when there was moonlight and

I saw there were no footprints ahead of me. At first I didn't believe my eyes but I backtracked, thinking he had given me the slip by crossing to the other side.

I found that the doctor's footprints ended at the cemetery fence.

I knew then that he was heading for the inn on the other side, the place from which he had kidnapped Maria and where I had seen him that evening. The proprietor worked for Schmidt. The doctor would find refuge at the inn. Probably Hermann was waiting. It was a good deal shorter to go through the cemetery and much safer.

I managed to pull myself to the top of the iron fence although I opened up the wounds in my hands and they bled profusely. I went over and let myself down again by dropping my feet until they touched a headstone, jumping the rest of the way into the drifted snow.

There was a line of naked trees against the sky, and I found they bordered a road. The ground is too hard to open graves in the winter months, but the cemetery roads are plowed so that the dead can be trucked to receiving vaults until spring.

I followed the road away from the fence, through a line of squat black tombs, wall to wall like the homes of the living that faced the cemetery gates.

I walked five minutes or so, and the road swung sharply to the left. When I had made the turn, the moon came from behind the clouds, and I saw Schmidt. I think he must have heard my step on the snow, which was packed hard as ice at that point. I don't think he knew until that moment that I was following. He wasn't more than fifty feet from me.

We were in the dark again, almost immediately, before either could use his gun. We were like two blind men, in the middle of that city of the dead, hunting each other, each waiting for the light of the moon yet fearing the other might use it first.

Schmidt fired the first shot without waiting for the moon. I never believed he had nerves but I think that's what happened. He must have aimed for the spot where he'd seen me standing. It was an error in judgment surprising in the Nazi doctor because I had been careful to put the wall of a tomb between myself and him.

I didn't fire back. I knew where he was and he hadn't located me.

The tombs paralleled the road. There was space behind them, between them and another marble row. The rest of the year it was a gravel path. I waded slowly through snow almost to my waist. I wanted to get in back of him. I didn't stop to think he might be vanishing along that road while I was playing cowboy and Indian. His job was to get away with the envelope and mine to catch him if I could.

But he didn't go. I can only guess why not. Perhaps he thought Walter was with me and that he was surrounded; a cemetery just before dawn can play queer tricks on a man's nerves. Maybe he thought his shot was already bringing a Russian patrol inside the gates.

At any rate, Schmidt was still standing in the middle of the road when I came out from behind the tombs. As soon as there was a little light, I dropped him with one bullet. He screamed like a child and the sound cascaded.

He wasn't dead when I reached him. I lifted his gun. I went through his pockets and found the Manila envelope.

Then the Russians drove through the gate, the one close by the spot where Schmidt and I had scaled the fence. They entered the cemetery as if they were children whistling and singing to keep the ghosts away. Even without the siren, we'd have known they were coming, even if they hadn't raced the engine like a hot-rod driver.

I jammed Schmidt's Homburg on his bullet head. I picked his broken gold-rimmed spectacles from the snow and started to push them on his face and then realized what I was doing and threw them away.

I grabbed the German by the scruff of his fat neck and dragged him off the road. I dragged him through the snow to the gate of a tomb. The gate opened, and I hauled him inside. I closed the gate and fumbled with the latch, unthinking, until I realized there is no lock on the inside of a tomb.

I sat in that tomb surrounded by the dead, my teeth chattering, and listened to the babble of a dying man.

Herr Doktor Wolfgang Schmidt, propped up against a coffin, laughed and pleaded and scolded out of his memory. The man who had never swerved an inch from his grotesque ideal during his lifetime, who never used sentiment or humanity or tenderness, called for his mother. Two or three times I found my bloody hands, the ones he'd smashed, closing round his stumpy throat to quiet him forever but I couldn't do it.

I heard the Russian car coming all the way from the

gate, the tires whirring as they skidded on the icy places, the whining of the engine. The spotlight took short cuts and once it lighted the inside of my prison, flooding through the grillwork in the gate like daylight. I drew back automatically although of course they couldn't see me. I lost my balance and fell on the marble floor and when I turned to pick myself up there was a grinning skull within reach of my hand.

They saw the marks in the snow as soon as they rounded the bend, the path I'd made in dragging Schmidt's body. They stopped almost in front of us and they saw the doctor's blood where he'd fallen.

I backed into the far corner and went down on all fours, behind an enormous copper casket, as the gate swung open.

"Here's one of them," a voice said in Russian. "He's still alive. Get him out of here."

"It's Schmidt," Anna Orlovska's voice said. "It's the German Schmidt."

"He must have crawled in here," the man's voice said. "The others must be close by."

There was a step on the marble floor, and the flashlight found me.

"What's back there?" the man's voice said.

"Nothing," the Countess Orlovska said. "There's nobody here. They must have headed for the fence again."

"All right," said the man. "Hurry up and get out of here. We haven't a minute to spare."

"It's okay with me," Orlovska said as the gate clanged shut again. "I don't like graveyards any more than you do."

❖

I waited until I could no longer hear the Russian car before I went out on the road. I was lucky in guessing the direction of Asztalos Sandor ut because Walter found me a few minutes after he had climbed the fence on Hiram's orders.

We made the Buda hills without trouble. The Russians must have been sure we were trapped in the cemetery because there were no roadblocks as there had been the night before. We never even saw a policeman.

We made the plane just as it braked to a stop, and Maria was there with Teensy and Walter's wife. We abandoned the car in the middle of the pasture.

The plane climbed over the trees and as soon as we had leveled off, the pilot gave us whisky. Hiram had lost a good deal of blood and he would be in the Vienna hospital for a long time, but he was conscious and took Marcel Blaye's envelope when I handed it to him.

While the others pretended to watch the countryside in the lightening dawn, I took Maria into my arms and kissed her.

Afterword

My father, who I called Bobby, but whose full name was Robert Bogardus Parker Jr., was first and foremost a newspaper man. He loved being where the action (what he called "the story") was, where the news was "being made." Most of my memories of him include an open newspaper or a typewriter. Even my baby photographs —1939 Budapest—age 14 months—show me on my father's lap looking at the camera while his eyes are downcast, reading a folded newspaper balanced on his knees.

The typewriter image is of an old, black, boxy Remington typewriter—a shiny black machine, the keys solid, round, and high. It sat in the base of its own case, the top having been lifted off and put aside. Bobby sat at a table, using the first fingers of both squarish hands to tap out "the story." Bobby, coffee cup on table, often cigarette in mouth, ripping a sheet of yellow paper out of the roller, wadding it up and throwing the ball of paper on the floor. ("Rurrripp, scrunch, fittttt!" Just like in the movies! Honest!) Within a few hours, the floor was littered with yellow paper balls.

The memories, however, are few. Most of these a
of summer visits to Morland, my paternal grandparent
farm in South Woodstock, Vermont. My father was
mainly an absent "presence" in the lives of my brother
Roby (Robert B. Parker III) and me and later, after my
parents divorced in 1947, a brief presence in the life of
my half-sister Lucci.

My father's first book was *Headquarters Budapest*,
published by Farrar & Rinehart in 1944. The jacket
copy gives his biography:

*Although still in his thirties, Robert Parker is one of
the few veteran correspondents who have seen the
war from the totalitarian side. He was with the
German Army on its march into Poland in 1939; he
rode with an armored division of Hungarians into
Sub-Carpathic Russia and saw Hungary, Rumania
and Bulgaria taken over by the Nazis. He also covered the Russian conquest of Bessarabia and, prior
to the current war, the revolution in Spain. He has
traveled widely in Germany and been in and out
of France and other Nazi-occupied countries many
times.*

*From 1939–41, he made his headquarters in
Budapest, Hungary, one of the best listening posts
in Europe. From the spring of 1942 up to a few
months ago, Mr. Parker was OWI [Office of War
Information] Chief in Turkey.*

*Robert Parker was born in Newark, N.J., and ed-
ucated at the Pingry School, Elizabeth, N.J., and
Union College, Schenectady, N.Y. He worked for a*

time on the staff of the Newark Evening Call *and the* Schenectady Gazette. *Upon his graduation from college, he worked for the* New York Journal, *from which in 1933 he transferred to The Associated Press. He was sent to Paris—and there began his eventful career as a foreign correspondent.*

Since it was still wartime, the jacket failed to mention that he, like many journalists, was also a member of the OSS (the predecessor to the CIA), an organization my mother referred to as "Oh, So Secret." My brother says that Bobby was in Shanghai when the Japanese invaded China in 1937, and I remember stories of his propaganda activities, such as putting Allied messages in prayer books in churches all over Europe, including Germany, and also tales of "Wild Bill" Donovan. During the war years, my father was involved in getting European Jews, including his assistant, Paul Vajda, out of prisons (and out of the country to safety, if possible). After my mother died, I found letters from people he had helped among her papers.

In 1946, we moved to Cincinnati, Ohio, where my father worked for Radio Station WLW. His daily 30-minute radio news program, "World News Analysis," aired at 11:00 P.M. (Not surprisingly, we children only heard it a few times, once when my mother was his guest.) On Sundays he and three other commentators, Jack Beall, Arthur Reilly, and Maj. General James E. Edmonds, all friends since their European days, shared a WLW news discussion panel called "The World Front."

In Ohio my parents divorced, and my mother, bro-

ther and I moved to Washington, D.C. Over the ne
nine years, my father owned an upstate New Yor
weekly newspaper that folded and a herd of cattle
that contracted hoof-and-mouth disease, and worked
for the *New York Daily News* and the United Nations
news bureau.

He wrote two more books: *Ticket to Oblivion* in
1950, and *Passport to Peril* in 1951. Published by
Rinehart & Co., they were also brought out in paper-
back editions by Dell. Reviewed as suspense novels
about European espionage, these books were praised
by reviewers as "suave, exciting, unusual, and thrilling."

I think those are the adjectives I would have used
as a teenaged daughter about my imagined father. I
feel it was a deep loss not to have known him better,
and longer.

I, for one, would have loved to know what he would
have thought or written about the fall of the Berlin Wall;
or the death of Alexander Litvinenko, the ex-KGB spy,
now MI6 agent, poisoned by radioactive polonium; or
about Radovan Karadzic, the Bosnian Serb leader-
turned-fugitive, wanted for international war crimes,
who, until he was finally arrested, lived right in Bel-
grade for a decade disguised as an eccentric monk-like
practitioner of alternative medicine.

My father died of a heart attack in 1955, just short
of his fiftieth birthday. His was a short life of accom-
plishment at an early age, a hard-hitting, heavy-drinking,
heavy-smoking, stress-filled existence. It was a life of
constant deadlines of all sorts. In many ways he lived

e life of his fictional protagonists, and like theirs, his asn't always a happy one.

During the war years, though, Bobby was just where he wanted to be—where the story was, in a period of great historical upheaval in the world.

Daphne Wolcott Parker Hawkes
Princeton, NJ

Get Hard Case Crime by Mail...
And Save 50%!

☐ **YES! Sign me up for the Hard Case Crime Book Club!**

As long as I choose to stay in the club, I will receive every Hard Case Crime book as it is published (generally one each month). I'll get to preview each title for 10 days. If I decide to keep it, I will pay only $3.99* — a savings of 50% off the standard cover price! There is no minimum number of books I must buy and I may cancel my membership at any time.

Name: _____

Address: _____

City / State / ZIP: _____

Telephone: _____

E-Mail: _____

☐ **I want to pay by credit card:** ☐ VISA ☐ MasterCard ☐ Discover

Card #: _____   Exp. date: _____

Signature: _____

Mail this page to:
HARD CASE CRIME BOOK CLUB
20 Academy Street, Norwalk, CT 06850-4032

Or fax it to 610-995-9274.
You can also sign up online at www.dorchesterpub.com.

* Plus $2.00 for shipping. Offer open to residents of the U.S. and Canada only. Canadian residents please call 1-800-481-9191 for pricing information.

If you are under 18, a parent or guardian must sign. Terms, prices, and conditions subject to change. Subscription subject to acceptance. Dorchester Publishing reserves the right to reject any order or cancel any subscription.